She laid her hand against his chest. "Feel it?"

The club's intense techno music carried a beat that practically thudded where she'd placed her hand. He was feeling more than that, though, and it had a lot to do with her enticing smile.

"What makes it better is a guy who gets me right off the bat."

Nate nodded. "Damned if anyone gets in your way."

"Hope that's okay with you—that I like to be in control." Though she sounded confident, there was a hint of hesitation in her eyes before she brought her face closer…almost touching his but not quite. "I don't kiss strangers in clubs."

"We're outside." A technicality, but he had to try.

"Funny." She paused again, shifting her weight from one foot to the other, and her right high-heeled shoe began scraping back and forth on the platform. Lifting her head, she trapped his gaze with an intense look that was flavored with amusement. "I didn't say that I don't kiss strangers in dark corners…or quiet halls with no one around."

"Do you?"

"In reality? Only when the situation calls for it," she said slowly, cautiously, as she turned and led him toward a deep, private shadow on the balcony.

"And in fantasy?"

"Always."

Books by Lisa Marie Perry

Harlequin Kimani Romance

Night Games

LISA MARIE PERRY

thinks an imagination's a terrible thing to ignore. So is a good cappuccino. After years of college, customer service gigs and a career in caregiving, she at last gave in to buying an espresso machine and writing to her imagination's desire. Lisa Marie lives in America's heartland, and she has every intention of making the Colorado mountains her new stomping grounds. She drives a truck, enjoys indie rock, collects medieval literature, watches too many comedies, has a not-so-secret love for lace and adores rugged men with a little bit of nerd.

Night
Games

Lisa Marie Perry

HARLEQUIN® KIMANI™ ROMANCE

For G—

Promise me you won't read this book until you're old enough to use *passion* correctly in a sentence.

Because I said so.

Recycling programs
for this product may
not exist in your area.

ISBN-13: 978-0-373-86348-8

NIGHT GAMES

Copyright © 2014 by Lisa Marie Perry

H HARLEQUIN®

Printed in U.S.A. www.Harlequin.com

Dear Reader,

Growing up a single-minded book lover, I resisted the appeal of American football. I really did put up a good fight. But since I come from a home filled with athletes and sports fanatics, one can guess how long that defiance lasted….

A battle on the gridiron has the power to turn strangers in the stands into friends or rivals. Men become warriors. Fans become an incredible force that urges them toward greatness.

But there's more to football than the game—especially for the Las Vegas Slayers. The ambitious, sexy and vivacious Blue daughters are putting their stamp on the very male world of football. In *Night Games,* competitive Charlotte Blue and jaded Nate Franco take risks, break rules, give in to passion *and* set off a chain of events that shake up Sin City.

I'm excited to introduce you to The Blue Dynasty, and I hope you'll enjoy Charlotte and Nate's story.

XOXO

Lisa Marie Perry

Chapter 1

"You look like the devil's sex puppet."

It wasn't the greatest compliment on her appearance, Charlotte Blue thought, but it sure wasn't the worst. "Thank you," she hollered across the curb to Josephine de la Peña—aka Joey—who stood waiting near the Rio's entrance. Only in Sin City—and only coming from her best friend—could "sex puppet" be taken as a favorable comment.

Not giving the chauffeur a chance to circle the vehicle and open her door, Charlotte had stepped out and paused at the BMW sedan's lowered front-passenger window to tip the man, a silent thanks to him for politely ignoring the fact that she was the subject of hot breaking-news debate on every sports radio station he'd attempted to listen to during the drive. Now, as he bid her a good evening with a touch to the visor of his cap, he *not*-so-politely slid his eyes to the golden-brown cleavage displayed by the deep V-neckline of her dress.

She'd almost chosen a more modest outfit, a tamer hairstyle. She'd come *this close* to ditching tonight's Las Vegas Slayers team party. In the back of her mind she'd been a little fearful that a woman intruding into a boys' club—which the National Football League undoubtedly was—shouldn't waltz into it dressed as sin in stilettos. But the getup was an invitation to a high-stakes dare she'd made with herself: *I dare you to take what you want...what you've earned.*

There were few things Charlotte enjoyed more than a good dare.

Hurrying to join Joey for preparty drinks at VooDoo, she was glad she'd covered her insecurity with the brand of confidence that only a gauzy scarlet dress and chocolate diamonds could provide. After all, a newly hired NFL assistant athletic trainer shouldn't skip meet-ups.

The reality that she had landed a shot at bringing her sports-medicine experience to a professional arena still hadn't fully registered. Pushing for aggressive reorganization— from administrative cleanup to fresh acquisitions—the new owners had preached to the media about wanting change. But Charlotte, who'd taken her bumps playing high school football and paid her dues training players for two NCAA teams, had still been rejected—twice. Then at the close of the Slayers' minicamp, just when she was ready to give up her pursuit of the job, she was offered a position. No wooing, no frills, just a take-it-or-leave-it open door to the gig of her dreams. And she was expected to be better than perfect.

According to the fresh headlines of major sports networks, she had three strikes against her: she was a woman, she was a *young* woman and the team's new owners were her parents, which screamed nepotism.

Thank the Lord this wasn't baseball, because three strikes didn't count her out.

Joey didn't wait for Charlotte to meet her on the curb before she jabbed her cane on the ground and limped with impressive speed toward the entrance, calling over her shoulder, "*Vamanos!* Gotta hustle before all the good tables, drinks and men are gone!"

Charlotte laughed, quickening her step and letting the oversize sheer bell sleeves of her dress flutter in the light wind. The red-and-purple glory of the Rio glowed against the dark sky that was illuminated with the lights of the Strip. She enjoyed what this city had to offer, but next week, right at the height of summer, training camp in Mount Charleston would be her home away from home.

Hot on Joey's Christian Louboutin heels, Charlotte said, "Let's divide and then we'll conquer our objectives. You snag a table, I'll order the drinks—rum and Diet Coke's still your drink of the week, right?—and we'll both scope out men."

"Could it be you're on the lookout for fling potential, too?" Though petite with an elfin face, Joey had a huge personality—and never minced words.

"I'm only looking, not touching. Camp's coming up and I really don't need the trouble."

"Oh, Lottie. If done right, a fling is *anything but* trouble." Joey led Charlotte to the entrance of VooDoo Lounge. "Where should we stake out? Indoors, outdoors, upstairs, downstairs?"

"Indoors downstairs for starters. I want to relax and savor my beer." Body heat, the mingling of spicy cologne and musky perfume, and the deep pulse of music confronted Charlotte as she followed her friend inside the dimly lit nightclub and began weaving through the crush of people. "By the way, I know what a fling is."

"Then you know it doesn't come with expectations and strings attached and everything else that falls under the trouble category. For a straight shooter who's always been about beating the odds, you sure play it safe when it comes to guys. I blame Wade. All I'm saying is if the same ol', same ol' disappoints over and over again, try something new. Think of the world as a bar. Why commit yourself to plain beer when you can have a shot of something new? Oh, found a table!" Joey took off in a blur of teal-colored chiffon with her cane tap-tap-tapping on the floor, leaving Charlotte no choice but to chase after her.

"Hey, I thought you were getting the drinks," Joey said when Charlotte claimed the chair opposite her and dropped her Fendi handbag onto the table. "Fine, I'll go."

Charlotte swiftly swiped Joey's cane from its perch on the seat of the chair between them. "No, you don't. I'll get the booze, but not until you hear this."

Joey muttered a creative expletive and Charlotte fought a smile. "FYI, I was over Wade the second he forbade— oh, yeah, *forbade*—me to take the Slayers' offer." Wade Eddington had used her to network in the NFL, promote his luxury-hotel chain and schmooze his suit-and-tie acquaintances with box-seat tickets before the Slayers franchise had even officially changed hands. The moment she'd shared with him the big news that hadn't been leaked to the media until tonight, he'd given her an ultimatum: give up her spot on the training staff or give him up.

That ultimatum had infuriated her, and so did Joey's accusation that Charlotte was incapable of taking a personal risk. She and Joey had been friends for three years, since the day Joey had caused a ruckus at the stadium's Slayers Club Lounge, complaining about her beyond-well-done prime-rib sandwich and saying she deserved to fill her belly with a good meal and see some football to forget how messed up it was that she'd been transferred to federal desk duty in Las Vegas after being pulled from a field job on Capitol Hill.

Charlotte, sick of being stood up, had taken satisfaction in giving away her no-show boyfriend's ticket and preferred bottle of Pinot Noir to a stranger, and she and Joey had been cool ever since. It was time to find out if her bestie could take what she dished out.

Charlotte folded her arms across her chest. "Have *you* had a fling this summer?"

"Uh, it's a bit more difficult for someone like me. What man wants a romp with a three-legged woman?"

"Don't say that, Joey." Truth be told, Joey was fortunate that the burden of a cane was the only lasting damage from the bullet lodged in her hip, and Charlotte didn't think it healthy for her friend to use her injury as an excuse to miss out on life.

Lightening the mood, and not one to let Joey get down on herself, she quipped, "Bet you a crisp hundred there's a *hawt* brother out there itching to get a three-legged woman."

Joey laughed, then, sobering, said, "Well, he may be 'out there,' but until he comes into this nightclub, I'm out of luck. Now *please* move your ass and get those drinks. I'm parched."

"You're horny and frustrated." Charlotte leaped up, grabbed her bag and dashed into the crowd before her friend could whack her with her cane.

At the crowded bar, Charlotte waited for a space to open up. She glanced back to her table and saw a man was already proffering Joey a drink. Clearly there was no shortage of men in Vegas interested in Mexican bombshells.

A woman vacated a barstool and Charlotte slid onto it, only to find no one manning the bar. A couple of young men with bottles of Dos Equis in tow bumped into her as they jostled each other for a spot at her elbow. At her firm headshake they grunted their "It's all goods" and moved on to a pair of women with flatironed hair and heavy eye shadow who appeared to be sopping up male attention like human sponges.

With a sigh, Charlotte inspected the front of her dress for damage. One camera snap of her looking disheveled would no doubt give her TMZ notoriety and the chew-up-spit-out sports media would be hungry for more—as if a beer-stained dress or even imperfect lipstick carried more urgency and importance than the fact that the Slayers had acquired three of last season's first-round draft picks and had snatched up a championship-winning quarterback just one day after his free agency had been announced. Not to mention that the injured safety the league had written off as a fallen star was in better health, in mental control, and come September would be in a silver-and-blood-red Slayers uniform—and Charlotte couldn't wait.

She took a moment to retrieve her compact and check her makeup. Beyond her own reflection in the small circle mirror was a pair of intense eyes…watching her. Snapping the compact shut, she whirled on her stool and silently confronted the man who lingered at the edge of the bar like a tall bronze-toned sculpture of muscle and lust and instant temptation.

At his quick wink all of her body heat redirected to pool deep in her belly. An unsteady breath escaped her lips before she could manage to string together a coherent sentence. "Need a mirror?" she uttered lamely, holding up the compact.

For the love of touchdowns, whatever you do, don't smile at me.

The corner of his perfectly kissable mouth tipped up in

the suggestion of a smirk that sent the ball of lava-hot intensity inside Charlotte to dip even lower. Confounded at such an involuntary reaction to a stranger, she fell into an old nervous habit, wiggling her right foot back and forth.

"No, thanks," he said, moving behind the bar.

Of course he would be the bartender. Olive-brown skin, a burr haircut and what looked like a few days' growth of stubble—he probably made an incredible income on what he took home in tips every night from women who weren't immune to his in-your-face appeal.

The things this man was doing to her rationality were downright dangerous. And for once she didn't even think about whether or not he would be welcomed into her family circle. The only men her parents *had* approved of were the ones they'd set her up with. A long line of plain, generic-labeled beer bottles. Already this guy, a shot of something dark and exotic, was something refreshingly different.

Maybe Joey *was* onto something. Still, Charlotte wasn't a girl for snap decisions and wasn't about to take on the first all-right-looking…okay, lip-bitingly hot…man who tossed her a crumb of attention. Everything—including flirting with a guy who had trouble written on every sexy square inch of him—required precision. She'd had her fill of heartache. Control mattered above anything else. "So. How well do you know your way around a cocktail?"

Intrigue and appreciation danced in dark eyes that reminded her of espresso and dark chocolate and everything that was forbidden but too delicious to resist. "I do all right."

Was that a hint of arrogance she detected in his tone? Or was he laying down a challenge? The natural-born competitor in her took the bait. "Got skills, then?"

"Mad skills." His tone was colored with a touch of humor. One point in his favor. He strode toward her, the sleek bar between them. "What's your pleasure?" His rich, deep voice traveled over her like a flutter on her skin.

"Beer, actually. It may be basic but I like it." It was the truth. She appreciated anything from dry martinis to whiskey sours to brandy cocktails, but she knew what to expect from no-frills beer.

"No matter what, you go for what you want."

Charlotte tipped her head and felt her dark brown tendrils tumble heavily over one shoulder, exposing the side of her neck to the room's heat. "Is that what beer says about the person drinking it?"

"It's what I say about you."

To hell with beer. She took pride in being tough to predict and define—something that people like Wade and her own family weren't comfortable with. "I want something…new."

"When did you decide that?"

"Just now."

Charlotte's eyes played over the broad span of his shoulders straining against his pristine white button-down shirt as he reached for a glass. For one dangerously weak moment she considered leaning across the bar to run her hands over his head and feel the spiky ends of his aggressively cut hair against her fingers.

Before she could do more than ogle him, he handed her a martini glass. That almost-smirk remained in place. "Maybe this will satisfy your need to be out of the ordinary."

Charlotte lifted the glass to her lips but didn't drink. "What is this?"

"A Sexy Devil martini. If you like cranberry, you'll love this. If not…try it anyway."

She sampled the strawberry garnish before sipping the drink. The flavor of cranberry vodka with an undertone of tart lemon tingled her taste buds. "Hmm. I like it." She flicked her tongue over her bottom lip to catch a droplet of the liquid, and his mouth turned serious in response.

Suddenly her thoughts were at war. *Order Joey's rum and Coke already. Give him your phone number. Concentrate on tonight's team party. Go book a room—you're at the Rio for heaven's sake!*

A text message from Joey was the nudge she needed.

I send you off for drinks and you find Adonis himself. That's talent, woman.

Charlotte glanced back at the table, caught her friend's sly shooing gesture before Joey leaned flirtatiously toward the man now sitting with her. Charlotte's voice was huskier than she'd ever heard it as she slipped her phone into her bag, dropped a twenty on the counter and said to the bartender, "Thanks for my Sexy Devil martini." She hopped off the stool, and someone immediately took it. "Free to take a break?"

The grin he'd been wrestling with finally broke, lighting up a face that she had mistakenly doubted could get any more attractive. He leisurely made his way to her, then pointed at a man behind the bar in a dark shirt and slacks who was prepping to wow a group of women with a round of VooDoo's famous Witch Doctors. "*I'm* not a bartender. My friend Clay is. And as you can see, he's got talent, but I prefer mixing my own drinks."

Her heartbeat kicked up at the realization. The unspoken challenge egged her on, urged her to do what everyone, it seemed, thought she couldn't. Ultimately, though, *she* was in control and wasn't about to do anything she didn't want to.

"Good." With a crook of her finger she beckoned him to follow her.

She wouldn't be long. Joey'd be fine. She had company.

This was going to go too far. Nate Franco knew it but still didn't miss a step as he let the siren in a red dress lead him up the stairwell to the nightclub's upper outdoor balcony. The goal had seemed simple enough earlier that evening when he'd gotten behind the wheel of his Benz and shot down the road, leaving in his wake the Lake Las Vegas mansion that his family had turned into a battleground. Make himself inaccessible to his family, stay at the Rio for the night, hit up VooDoo for an hour, tops, just for a drink in the midst of a few hundred people who, thankfully, were strangers—not family. A casual hookup wasn't what he'd come here for, but it was a fantastic alternative to playing peacemaker.

Selfishly, he wanted to find some peace for himself. At the close of the Slayers' last minicamp, he'd taken a few weeks of personal time—much of which was spent refereeing his brother and their father, whose fiancée, Bindi, was a twenty-nine-year-old blonde bug buzzing in his ear nonstop about *her* future and how the Franco family losing control of the Las Vegas Slayers was affecting *her* life. The new owners hadn't yet flicked him from the training staff and he was the last of the Francos affiliated with the team. So naturally her focus had turned to him and what he intended to do to fix the situation.

He'd only managed to hold off the crazy by channeling his anxiety into what he most enjoyed: the company of a beautiful woman. A weekend in Key Largo with a tiki-bar waitress had taken off some of the edge, but what was left still weighed him down.

Contrary to what many believed, there was no "off-season" in professional football. Several days from now it would be back to the training facility that he knew better than his own luxury condo in the city, back to rehabilitation and practice, back to going toe-to-toe with coaches and players. Back to work.

He hadn't been canned yet, but how long would it last? His older brother, Santino, hadn't bowed out gracefully when their father had sold the Slayers franchise. Nate couldn't blame the injured-into-retirement tight end for taking the loss of his birthright personally. The heir apparent had gotten screwed. Both he and Nate had watched their legacy get signed away, along with all the possibilities that came with it, and the new owners, who his father claimed had aggressively convinced him to sell the team to them, were trigger-happy when it came to hiring and, especially, firing.

Right now Nate had a fragile position of power as an outsider who was inside the gates. But he didn't need his brother to remind him that the career he'd taken for granted could be yanked from him at the slightest misstep. No question the Blues, the intimidating husband-and-wife duo who'd purchased the Slayers, would be watching him closely—so he would proceed carefully, earn a rapport, figure out where loyalties lay and who to trust.

For Nate, proving that the Blues had practically stolen a multimillion-dollar ball club from the Francos was personal.

But who better to help him take the edge off than the lady in front of him? Damn, had he ever seen a pair of legs so finely toned and smooth looking?

"Now, *this*—" the distraction in red sent him a nod over her shoulder "—is where it's at."

The club's balcony was jammed with dancing patrons carrying drinks—and cameras. Subtly, he shifted to the right and circled a hand around her wrist, drawing her to a less crowded spot. He resembled his brother closely enough to have been mistakenly asked for his autograph more than once and didn't want what short time he had to spare with this woman to be invaded by family complications.

In a couple of hours he'd be at one of the city's most exclusive VIP rooms celebrating the start of another season—this one free of lockout uncertainties but still not without Slayers-style drama. At the minicamps, he'd seen more new faces than familiar ones, and over a third of all the players who would survive the hell on grass that was training camp would see their fantasies of bringing it to a pro game go up in smoke.

On some level he could commiserate. If he didn't strike the right balance between lying low enough and being outgoing enough he'd be cut, too. The owners were still adjusting the coaching and training staff. A new assistant trainer had been announced today. He'd have to be sure to introduce himself. But his father's fiancée's latest tantrum had drained his patience to the point where he'd resolved to unplug himself from work and family and had mindlessly gambled away over $200 in the casino after checking into the hotel's Cariocas Suite.

"Why'd you invite me out here?" he asked, leaning close to the woman's ear.

Her shrug rewarded him with a hint of fruity perfume. "Just trying something new," she said in a point-blank way that made him believe, when it came to this lady, what he saw was what he'd get. And he liked what he saw. She was fit, had hair as dark as ink—hair he wanted to lose his hands in—and equally dark eyes that were more thoughtful than serious.

A passing couple bumped her but she made sure not to brush against him. This was a woman determined to remain in control. "Why don't we take the path less trav-eled here," she said. "Did you come to this club to meet the person you're going to marry?"

"No," he said without a hitch.

"Neither did I." The relief shone on her face. "Consider this a fantasy, with no real expectations. So what if you and I drop the formalities and the whole list of Dating 101 get-to-know-ya questions?"

His brain was apparently slow to catch up. No woman he'd ever touched had laid it out quite like this. There was always some introduction, some prelude to sex, offering the illusion that he and she were interested in more than purely superficial pleasure. "I'm a part of your…fantasy?"

"Only if you want to be." She waved an arm, indicating the Vegas cityscape. "It all starts with perfecting the mo-ment. Great vibe, amazing background, music with bass you can feel here." She laid her hand against his chest. "Feel it?"

The club's intense techno music carried a beat that prac-tically thudded where she'd placed her hand in the center of his chest. He was feeling more than that, though, and it had a lot to do with her enticing smile.

"What makes it better is a guy who gets me right off the bat."

Nate nodded. "Damned if anyone gets in your way."

"Hope that's okay with you—that I like to be in con-trol." Though she sounded confident, there was a hint of hesitation in her eyes before she brought her face closer… almost touching his but not quite. "I don't kiss strangers in clubs."

"We're outside." A technicality, but he had to try.

"Funny." She paused again, shifting her weight from one foot to the other, and her right high-heeled shoe began scraping back and forth on the platform. Lifting her head, she trapped his gaze with an intense look that was flavored with amusement. "I didn't say that I don't kiss strangers in dark corners…or quiet halls with no one around."

"Do you?"

"In reality? Only when the situation calls for it," she said slowly, cautiously, as she turned and led him toward a deep, private shadow on the balcony.

"And in fantasy?"

"Always."

Chapter 2

*A*lways. The word sizzled right through Nate's body, controlling him as if he were held prisoner by unbreakable strings. The Key Largo tiki-bar waitress had been more freaky than flirtatious, more calculating than classy. She hadn't gripped him the way this woman did.

Were they still playing along in her fantasy, or had they crossed the line to reality, where being with her for even another minute wasn't guaranteed?

Uncertainty stirred his adrenaline. He sensed that he didn't have the luxury of time. He needed to find out her motives and intent, her vulnerabilities…and oh, yeah, what she had on underneath that thin red gift wrap.

Playing it the way she'd laid it out seemed the best way to go. He needed to be cool. Even if his pants were ablaze.

"I have the Cariocas Suite," he said. Now was the best moment to let her know that he liked to be in control, too.

"It's more private than any dark corner or empty hall in this building. Want a fantasy with me? Then let's go."

Nate moved with purpose, snaking his fingers over hers and switching directions to get them to his suite the fastest. In the elevator she watched him closely before inquiring, "Why'd you hold my hand when we left the lounge?"

He stepped closer, until she was snug in a back corner of the elevator with nothing to focus on but his eyes, his words. "I wanted anyone who looked at us to know that you chose me."

When the doors opened, revealing his quiet floor and the promise of what would happen once enclosed in his suite, she stepped out ahead of him, then asked over her shoulder, "When you saw me at the bar, did you know I'd end up in your room?"

"Know? Nope. But surprises keep life interesting, don't they?" At the tightness in his voice, he softened the tension crackling between them with a quick curve of his lips. He unlocked the door and pushed it open. "Technically, you aren't in my room."

A fact he wanted to change *now*.

"You're in a quiet hall, with nobody around but me," he added, and saw her eyes widen in response.

"And now…" she moved toward him, then past him just into the suite's foyer "…I'm in your room."

Nate rounded on his heel and filled the doorway, his hands planted on the frame above his head.

Her gaze coasted over him, taking in his height and form. "Well, are you going to kick me out?"

Moments danced by before he dropped his hands and reached her in two steps. "Hell, no." Then his mouth crushed against hers.

She hooked her arms around his neck and hauled herself up, bringing her taut abdomen and supple breasts flush with his body. Her mouth opened without coaxing, and he indulged in swiping his tongue across her top row of teeth. She dropped back.

Nate fisted her bell sleeves, pulling her closer. One more tug on her sleeves and she was pressed to him again.

She wriggled out of his grasp and walked her fingers down the front of his shirt, undoing buttons along the way. At the last button she paused, teasingly shifting her weight from one foot to the other with those round dark eyes on his. "One question, though. What do people call you?"

"Nate."

"People call me Lottie." The final button was freed, and the sides of his shirt fell open.

What would he do if he couldn't touch her bare flesh? He wasn't going to find out, that was for damn sure.

Nate brushed her hair back from her face, felt the tendrils slide over his skin, then let his fingers drift over her collarbone before he plucked the oversize sleeves off her shoulders and drew the barely there garment down her body.

Lottie arrowed up, a squeal bubbling out as he continued to tug until she was down to silver lacy V-string panties and a deep red bra with half cups that offered soft, smooth breasts he wanted to lose himself in. She nimbly brought her leg up and fastened it around his waist, then hoisted herself onto him, the intimate contact eliciting a groan from deep within him.

Another flash of her smile, and he was ready to pin her to his king-size bed then and there.

"I'm looking forward to hearing you moan and scream, Lottie."

"Give me a reason to, and I will."

Control kept Charlotte grounded…sane. In her world, losing control meant welcoming chaos. But hot *day-um,* she felt herself delighting in following Nate's lead as he touched and whispered and coaxed and reminded her exactly how good it felt to just let go.

Over ten years had passed since her last true fun-only fling. Along the way she'd become accustomed to committed relationships that had pleased her parents. At least when those fell apart, she never had to worry about her mother and father blaming her for choosing the wrong man.

A relationship was the last thing she wanted, and the man skimming his hands down her back now was more than capable of giving her what she *did* want: no-hassle passion.

Nate took her mouth again, and the sensation intensified when he cupped her booty with both hands and squeezed.

Hit with stray concerns of whether he thought her butt was too fleshy or not fleshy enough, she whispered, "Nothing special there."

"I think you're wrong about that." For emphasis he gave her a firm tap, then, with a low rumble of laughter, soothed the spot with a gentle stroke. "Nice jiggle."

Was she actually in a suite at the Rio, down to her undies and heels, having her booty tapped by a panty-meltingly hot not-a-bartender?

Nate shifted her against him and she felt a thick ridge of hard flesh at the juncture of her thighs. Um. Yeah. This was *so* happening.

He set her on her feet and led the way past a lavish sitting area, and when she paused to kick off her shoes, she looked up and saw the city twinkling outside the wall of windows.

"Lottie?" He stood in the doorway of what must be the suite's bedroom.

Charlotte glanced back at him, then again toward the nighttime view. Go big or go home, right?

Before she had a chance to change her mind, she reached behind her and unsnapped her bra. The bold move felt more as though she'd freed herself from chains as opposed to delicate lace. "Come get me here."

Nate muttered a dirty curse that seemed to stroke all her erogenous zones at once, and rushed her, taking her with him to the sofa. He fit his hands over her breasts, scraping his fingernails across her nipples until she cried out and gripped his sides with her knees.

With a push to his chest, she urged him backward onto the sofa, rising up to straddle his hips. "Let's even out the playing field and get you just as naked as I am."

He drew a fingertip down from the side of her face to her nipple. The movement was slow, almost too sweet for an encounter between two strangers who after tonight would never see one another again.

She interrupted his exploration to creatively reverse her straddle and scoot up his torso, backing her butt up close to his face. She unhooked his belt and diligently pushed both his pants and boxer briefs down his hips until she was rewarded with the sight of his erection.

Nate caught her waist and slid her up higher. Bent over him, she felt totally bared, erotically exposed...and at the mercy of his mouth when he swirled his tongue over the flimsy fabric between her legs.

And her phone buzzed.

Or was that her? The sudden damp heat of his mouth had her eyes crossing and she clenched her jaw so tightly she might've chipped a tooth.

Another buzz. Definitely her phone. The sound stopped, only to resume several seconds later. The caller wasn't giving up.

Charlotte pushed away from Nate. "I have to get that."

"Ignore it. Please."

"I'm ninety-nine percent certain who's calling, and she doesn't respond well to being ignored." Tuning out his protests, Charlotte ran all but naked—save a moist lacy V-string—to the foyer table where she'd deposited her handbag.

A swift glance at the caller ID on the phone's display confirmed that her mother was calling, no doubt irritated that her eldest child was late for the Slayers' party. Instantly her mother's name and number put priorities back into perspective, and with slightly unsteady hands Charlotte returned the phone to her bag. Playtime was over, but she wouldn't answer the call while still in Nate's suite— and topless.

She strode back into the sitting room.

"Mmm. You standing there in those diamonds with Las Vegas behind you is incredible."

If only he knew that part of her was still lost in their unexpected hookup and didn't want to leave unfulfilled. He was all ropey muscle stretched out on the sofa, ready to come and get her.

"This was interesting, Nate," she said, schooling her features into a calm expression. "But I've got to go now." As if to punctuate the announcement, her phone started convulsing in her bag again.

She averted her gaze, because the last thing she needed was to see her own disappointment mirrored in this man's eyes or to be persuaded to stay when she shouldn't.

"What was that, then, Lottie? An escape call?"

As if she *wanted* to escape this? "No, I didn't invent a reason to leave. I know how this looks, all right? But I got carried away with you and misjudged the time. I'm supposed to be somewhere else, Nate. Not here."

Wish I had no other place to be but *here.* Whoa. How had she so *totally* lost the focus she reserved for the job that meant everything to her? She didn't know this man, so why did the thought of breezing out of his life prickle painfully?

Charlotte sighed, watched him kick aside his underwear and step into his pants, his face etched with carefully controlled—but no doubt deep—disappointment. Seeing his muscles bunch triggered a reminder of how only moments ago he'd scooted her up his torso and licked her right through her V-string. Her nipples pebbled at the memory, growing even harder as he looked her way.

Sighing, she turned to find her bra, mentally patting herself on the back for maintaining the dignity—okay, stubbornness—to not hide her traitorously alert nipples.

"See, staying with you longer would only get in the way of something that I've *really* wanted for a long time, Nate."

"We can't have that."

The mournful note in his voice nearly shook her where she stood. Could letting her go really affect him, when women probably moved through his life like fallen leaves down the road, and there were likely dozens still partying in VooDoo who could easily take her place? Could an instant connection—no matter how electric—matter that much to him? "Haven't you ever had a goal to push for, something that takes priority over everything else?" she asked thoughtfully.

"I do, as a matter of fact."

"And it's bigger, more important, than this thing between us, right?"

"Yeah," came the gravelly response. "It really is."

"You'll be all right." She pulled on her dress in record speed. Hoping for levity, she added, "That thing guys say happens to their anatomy after getting all worked up with no follow-through? Bull."

"You're killing me," he replied, escorting her to the door. Still shirtless. Still delicious.

"Maybe we'll see each other again."

"If I had your phone number, I could make sure we do, Lottie."

"Can't do that. If I give you my number, I'll be expecting you to call. Guess I'm needy that way. And I don't want to put you—or me—through that whole phone-call-expectation thing. We know each other's first names, so if we're meant to find one another again, it'll happen. If not, so be it."

"So be it," he echoed in a voice that was controlled but couldn't disguise his regret. "Goodbye."

With a wiggle of her fingers, Charlotte hurried out of the suite and away from hands down the hottest *almost-a-fling* of her life.

Chapter 3

Halfway down the stairs Charlotte paused, pressing herself against the handrail to avoid the stampede of patrons rushing past her. Faceless, indistinct, unmemorable—the whole lot of them. The one person she saw each time she blinked her eyes was the man she'd just left in the hotel's Cariocas Suite. Not wanting to loiter on his floor waiting for the elevator, she'd rushed to the stairs and hoped to catch the elevator on a lower level. As she picked her way through the crowds to VooDoo, she reminded herself that he was just a stranger.

But that nagging little thing called guilt told her she ought to be ashamed of herself for not being up-front with him. He'd asked for her phone number and she'd turned him down because she didn't want expectations. Or so she'd said.

Well, *that* wasn't really true. She'd grown up popular—an athlete who many people said had been lucky to inherit her mother's Miss Nevada beauty, but she was cursed to take after her "my way is the *only* way" father. Charlotte did what she wanted and had cared less about her looks and more about playing football, getting dirty and generally defying anyone who tried to stop her from marching to her own tune.

Attention from boys—flowers and phone calls—had never mattered a lick. Now that she was well past grown and had kissed her share of frogs that had turned out to be men who were insults to amphibians everywhere, she wasn't about to expect anything from a man.

Letting Nate think she was the clingy type who waited for the phone to ring was a cop-out, all right. But wasn't that better than the absolute truth? She was *the* Charlotte Blue, whose name, at this very moment, was being dragged through sports-media mud. The truth was too personal to share with a stranger. And for all she knew, judging by how effortlessly smooth he was, interested women were a dime a dozen and, like plenty of the people sidestepping her on the stairwell now, he'd come to Las Vegas for play only.

Yes, she was ready to finally move forward and put Wade behind her. But even though it made no sense, she could tell from how Nate had made her go from zero to horny in two seconds flat that he was no ordinary frog. Give somebody like that an inch and he'd be liable to take her heart. Which wasn't an option. A practically anonymous hookup was one thing. But a recurring fling with Nate would be a terrible mistake.

Are you sure about that?

That nagging thing called guilt sure sounded a lot like the annoying thing called doubt that was buzzing in her mind's ear like an unswattable fly.

"I'm sure," she muttered, flicking her finger next to her ear as if to thump doubt to oblivion. Charlotte stopped short and through the crowd saw Joey still sitting at their table. Alone. Maybe the guy who'd been so attentive to her earlier was in the restroom or off somewhere making a phone call or…

Joey propped her elbows on the table and dropped her face into her hands with enough force to toss her hair forward.

"Dang," Charlotte whispered, already steamed at the man who'd lifted her friend's hopes only to drop her the second he realized she wasn't perfect. She wasn't making assumptions; she knew in her gut what the score was.

Fishing into her purse for a twenty, Charlotte wiggled her way to the bar again. "Rum and Diet Coke, please. Quickly."

Armed with the drink, she returned to the table and set the glass down. "I think you ordered this?" she said to Joey, who was still cradling her head.

Startled, her friend dropped her hands and eyed her with incredulity. "Forever ago. You're still here?"

"Yes, and I feel really sucky for skipping out with—"

"Adonis."

Charlotte conceded and grinned. "His name's Nate. Forget about him, though. It's not gonna fly with us."

Joey took a gulp of the drink. "Too bad. He turned your head, *chica,* and that's saying a lot."

"Oh, yeah?"

"Yeah. You're…what's the best way to describe it?"

"Particular?"

"*Loca* is more like it." Joey polished off the drink, then took a deep breath. "What's wrong with him, then? Let's hear it."

Charlotte pulled up the chair beside Joey, removed her friend's cane and sat. "Nothing," she said, steadying the cane across her lap. "That's what's wrong with him. He appears perfect, which is obviously not possible. He's not a good candidate for a short-and-sweet fling, you know."

Although he *had* several minutes ago had that magic mouth on her underwear.

"Hmm. I also know you appear flushed and your lips have that 'I've been had' look. Just sayin'."

Blasted Joey. The woman had tossed back at least two drinks and was still probably the most observant person in the room. Insane levels of perception and know-it-all must be prerequisites for DEA agents. "Then I'll fix my makeup in the car on the way to the party. Let's go, Jo."

"'Let's'? I'm not—"

"Coming to the party? Yes, you are, and don't even think about passing this up. I'm not leaving you here to wallow in the Land of the Glow Sticks." To emphasize her point, she subtly tilted her head toward the group nabbing the table behind theirs. Both men and one of the women were waving around the crayon-bright neon sticks. "Definitely time for a change of milieu."

Joey shook an ice cube from the glass and popped it into her mouth. "Two different men came up to me tonight, Lottie. Two. And they both lost their *huevos* and ran off once they found out that not only do I not dance, but I can't walk more than three steps without this." She put down the glass and grabbed the cane from Charlotte's hands.

"Maybe they realized you'd bop them with it if they tried anything ungentlemanly."

Joey's laugh lit her face, and Charlotte knew she'd won this round. "Put that cane to use and let's get out of here. Pop's probably wondering where I am now."

Leaving VooDoo, they took a few minutes to freshen up in the ladies' room at the Rio before Charlotte called her private driver. It went without saying that news camera crews and reporters and paparazzi were already swarming around the party, and it was unlikely she could slink into it without someone snapping at least one shot of her with smudged lipstick. For her mother's and father's sakes, she would make an impression at tonight's party that they could both be proud of. Or she'd at least *try* to.

Marshall and Temperance Blue were big believers in the whole "reap the rewards of hard work" philosophy, which was why her father had finally acknowledged that Charlotte's determination and proven professional victories made her a viable candidate for the assistant athletic trainer position. If not for her blood and sweat—and the tears that she was now an expert at hiding—she would've been overlooked for the job simply because her parents had never really, fully accepted that their firstborn daughter was more warrior than princess and sometimes wanted to be rough-and-tumble and untamed when they thought she should be more gentle.

All eyes were on her, all right. Particularly Marshall's and Tem's. Just that morning, Charlotte had gotten up at dawn for a jog and found her mother's neatly written Post-it on the door to the Bellagio villa bedroom she shared with her sister Martha.

L—

Much to do before the get-together. See you tonight. Please no Charlotte Slipups.

—T

A "Charlotte Slipup" ranged from running her mouth off to thumbing her nose at authority and was pretty much any action that aggravated her mother or provoked her father's heartburn episodes and caused him to reach for the antacids he carried in the inside pockets of his tailor-made jackets. Though she had two younger sisters who'd both experienced rebellion of varying shades, her own so-called slipups were the ones that her parents always seemed to recall and hold on to like ammunition to shoot down her ambitions.

No, Charlotte would never come close to perfect. But this time she wouldn't land on her face. She'd worked her tail off to carve out a place for herself in the NFL, and she was going to reap the rewards of it by keeping her team fit for success. It would smooth things, though, to have respect—the media's, the team's…her family's.

"Cool down, Lottie," Joey said, noticing Charlotte's nervousness as they stepped out of the BMW and headed for the Bellagio. An escort greeted them with a smile and led the way into the hotel toward the Tower Ballroom, where the Slayers' party was probably in full swing.

There were flashes and clicks of cameras, shouts from reporters surging forth with microphones and eager questioning eyes. Charlotte remained silent, maintaining a neutral expression on her face as she walked—neither too slowly nor too quickly.

Once inside the ballroom she was greeted by upbeat music and some familiar faces. Almost immediately she was swept into the fray and joined in conversation with a few of her cousins who lived locally and then a few guys from the team whom she'd met previously at one meeting or another. Once she could break away, she and Joey located Marshall and Tem, surrounded by other well-dressed guests.

In a matter of months, since the official announcement that the Blues had acquired the Las Vegas Slayers franchise, her family had reached a new strata of fame. Some compared them to the Kardashians. The Blues were seeing a different level of attention than they had when an all-partied-out Martha had returned to school to become a publicist, or when Danica had sponsored a nonprofit organization dedicated to getting at-risk youths out of gangs and into the classroom. Thankfully, these items had been given some recognition earlier that week, when they'd been interviewed by the producers for a BET program that highlighted up-and-coming African-American families.

Charlotte doubted there would be much footage of her, since she'd already resigned as athletic trainer for the UNLV Rebels and the official statement announcing her hiring hadn't yet been released and at that time, while Danica was the newly minted general manager and Martha one of the team's new publicists, Charlotte had been the only Blue daughter who wasn't a part of the Slayers franchise. Afterward her mother had reprimanded her for being unapproachable simply because she'd refused to discuss her personal life with the interviewer and had been adamant about focusing only on her past achievements and hopes to eventually participate in the NFL's head-injury studies. But after today's news she'd likely be seeing that very same interviewer again for an update before the segment's airdate. "Excuse me, everyone. Just want to let the 'rents know I showed up after all."

"Charlotte." Her mother, coiffed and plucked and fresh as the fragrant jasmine and magnolias that filled the ballroom with their scent, folded her into a brief hug and murmured, "That dress is a little revealing, don't you agree?"

"You look nice, too, Ma."

"Oh, Lottie," Tem said, sounding put out. "You aren't just the team owners' daughter. You're a trainer. Have a care about how you interact with the men—"

"It's a party, Ma. Take a break from griping and have a glass of champagne or something." She ducked out of

Tem's grasp and said, "I invited Joey along. The more the merrier, right?"

"Josephine, you're always welcome," Tem said warmly, but shooting Charlotte a we're-not-finished look. "Help yourself to the food."

Joey wandered off to take immediate advantage of that offer, and Charlotte said to her father, "Pop, Kip Claussen's here, isn't he?"

"That's right," Marshall said, handing his wineglass to a nearby waiter. "You haven't met the new HC yet. Let's take care of that now."

He offered his elbow and they approached a broad-shouldered blond man who Charlotte pegged to be in his late forties. He could've just stepped out of the pages of *GQ* with his well-coordinated Armani suit and Cartier watch. He pointed his glass of Bacardi at Marshall as he said, "Aha! There's the man."

The men exchanged greetings in their equally booming voices, then addressed a trio from the offensive line who, though cleaned up in silk shirts and pressed slacks, appeared just as strong and ferocious as they did on the field. Finally, Charlotte barged into the conversation with "Kip, it's good to meet you. I'm Charlotte Blue."

Kip turned a pair of flummoxed blue eyes to her before raising his brows expectantly at Marshall as if to gibe, "Is she like this all the time? What a piece of work!"

At the unapologetic interruption, her father looked at her with an expression that was dashed with irritation. "Right, right, Kip. My daughter asked for you personally."

"Can I be flattered?" Kip's nonplussed look melted into what had to be his version of charm when dealing with the *gentler* sex. His mouth stretched into a white toothy grin that showed the man clearly wasn't used to smiling. "We're teammates, Coach. There's no need for flattery here," Charlotte said, sticking out her hand for a shake, which he didn't hesitate to provide. "You're a busy man, so it's expected that we've had a devil of a time getting together. I was really hoping to meet my new boss before training camp."

Marshall took that moment to stride off to parts of the room unknown.

"Kip, I thought I'd get to know you a bit. Find out who I'm working with. It'll be easier to get the particulars out of the way before we all come together in Mount Charleston."

Kip nodded to the mix of players and security personnel who'd been lingering quietly and they moved away. "Charlotte, let me be frank. I get the feeling Marshall and Temperance want to make a statement with this franchise. Out with the old. In with some changes. Marshall's the muscle and he's gonna do whatever the hell he wants. The media's calling it the 'Blue Dynasty.' My concern's that with this statement, they—and you—are overlooking the challenges you're going to face."

"My parents didn't hire me to make a statement," she objected, pausing to take a slim carrot stick from the tray of a passing server. "I know this won't be an easy job, but I'm the best person for it. I just happen to come with a different set of equipment than the rest of the training staff." She bit into the carrot with a smirk.

"Funny." Kip gestured with his glass for emphasis. "Funny's good. You'll need a sense of humor."

"Check."

"And balls. Bravado, I mean, of course."

"Check."

Serious now, Kip said, "Listen, Charlotte, an all-male locker room's a world away from what you're probably used to. Some of these guys around the league are creeps. They're not on the team because they're the nicest guys

on the planet but because they can play. They aren't looking forward to curbing how they talk and act because a
woman's been thrown into the mix."

She finished the carrot. "I'm not on this team to make
all these guys politically correct."

"You'll change your tune the second you hear a lame-
as-hell T & A joke."

"Come on, now. I don't discriminate. I'm insulted by
any lame-as-hell joke."

Pure surprise filled Kip's eyes, and after a moment he
nodded and took a swallow of his Bacardi. "Well, now that
we've got *those* particulars out of the way, what do you
want to know about me?"

"Lottie!"

Charlotte whirled around to see her sister pushing
through the clusters of guests. "Need you for a moment."

"Martha, I'm in the middle—"

"A party crasher's asking for you." Never one to let herself be put off, Martha jammed her hands on her hips and
frowned in a way that would've seemed childish and un-
attractive on anyone else. Dolled up in a blue-black dress
and high heels that showcased her gazelle legs, she said,
"Hi there. I'm Martha, the gal who'll be making all you
men look good." She took Kip's hand in a way that could
have been seen as cordial or licentious. "I'm a publicist.
And Charlotte's younger sister."

"Down, girl," Charlotte murmured to Martha. At
twenty-two, Martha was the "surprise" her parents had
had late in life—a fact she never got tired of flaunting.
She disengaged her sister's hand from Kip's. "Where's this
party crasher, and why didn't you let Pop know?"

"He wants you. Try not to get lost in his eyes." Martha
led the way to the built-in stage behind a curtain that was
nothing but dark nooks.

"Okay, this is a little weird…. What were you even doing back here, Martha?"

"Exploring."

Charlotte stepped around her sister to see Dex Harper waiting with his arms loose at his sides. Under direct orders, the new general manager—her sister Danica, who'd shot up the ladder as a talent-scout-turned-corporate-attorney—had relieved him of his QB duties with the Slayers and he'd taken the news very badly, very publicly. Notorious as the "blue-eyed badass" off the field, he'd racked up numerous fines over his four seasons with Las Vegas.

"Charlotte, I'm Dex Har—"

"I know who you are, Dex. What I don't know is what you think I can do for you. The GM and the owners' decision about your relationship with the team is final."

"It wasn't final when Marshall and Temperance turned your application down twice," Dex volleyed back, his eyes pleading. "That's what ESPN and Fox and every-damn-body is talking about tonight."

"I won't discuss my career with you."

"Look, Charlotte, your father's a stubborn bastard—"

"Hey!" Martha piped up.

"—but he can bend. Hear me out."

"As if *I* can give you a place on this team? Four seasons, Dex. Four to show you were worth what the previous front office spent on you, and you choked halfway through. All that talent and where'd it go?"

Dex glowered, but she wasn't close to backing down. "All of a sudden you got yourself a candy arm. Your on-field decisions, the incomplete passes? Laughable. My parents both want this team to be a contender, and you're not the quarterback to see us to that. The people who let you go believe you're too much of a liability."

"And your kicker, TreShawn Dibbs, isn't? He's a goddamn—" Dex exhaled harshly through his nostrils. "He's a train wreck, and the GM opened the gate to him."

"Dibbs's hiring has nothing to do with me. I'm one of the people who'll work to keep him healthy, that's all. You should be consulting with your agent to sign with another team—"

"No one's interested and you're wrong, Charlotte. All the crap that happened on the field—it's not on me. I swear that to you. I don't have a candy arm. I'm good, all right, and what I want is a chance to prove it under new leadership."

"So you're blaming your poor performance on the old administration? You're blameless?"

Martha's eyes darted back and forth between them, as if glued to a tennis match.

"Not blameless," he admitted. "I made a few effed-up decisions, didn't trust my gut. But I was a marked man, Charlotte, and I do have talent."

"Dex," Charlotte said carefully, firmly, "we have our quarterback."

With a glare, Harper turned and walked off, Martha following, determined to ensure the man who called their father a "stubborn bastard" found his way off the section of the premises that had been reserved for the Slayers' party.

Charlotte slipped back into the crowd again to find her father and notify him of the incident. Anyone who thought she'd landed any of her training jobs through nepotism was dead wrong. Her parents didn't approve of her dive into the front lines of male-dominated sports, and just like when she was a child who disobeyed their instructions, she had to deal with the consequences of her actions without them being her safety net. She'd learned that when a few boys on the high school football team had purposely plowed into her, fracturing her arm. In response, her parents had simply sat in the hospital waiting room while her arm was set in a cast, then asked whether she wanted to quit the team or not. She hadn't quit but had endured. So much so that she'd mastered the art of enduring.

Some called her parents' methods tough love; they called it teaching her responsibility and good common sense. Whatever it was, she knew she couldn't run to them for consolation when life didn't pan out as she hoped.

"Pop," she said, reaching up to tap Marshall on the shoulder. Outfitted in a gray Gucci Signoria suit, her father was big and bald and still radiated the powerful energy of a man who harvested physical and mental strength. Though he no longer competed as a bodybuilder, focusing instead on philanthropy, global investing and his glorious success as a shareholder of a billion-dollar power company, he made it an obsession to stay in top form. "Dex Harper was here. He had a few words for me, but he's gone now."

Marshall assessed her with a level stare. A shade or two darker than his deep brown skin tone, his irises gave no indication of what he was thinking. Like many of the men roaming this party tonight, he was no gentle giant. "What kind of words?"

"Nothing I couldn't handle." With that, Charlotte turned on her heel. What she wanted was to fill a plate, park it at a table and eat. No, first she wanted to say to her father, "See, I *can* hold my own!" and then eat.

"Charlotte!"

"Yo, Joey. Having a good time?"

Her friend wiggled her brows suggestively. "Not nearly as good as you're about to have, apparently. I should revoke your best-friend privileges for not dishing about your fling on Flamingo Road. You let me think nothing happened with you and that guy from the Rio."

Confused, Charlotte said, "That's the truth. We didn't—" she dropped her voice "—have sex."

Not *completely,* anyway.

"So if he was so wrong for you and not the guy you want an affair with, why'd you invite him to your team's party?"

"What?"

"Lottie, the jig is up! I saw him with my own eyes. In fact—" Joey took Charlotte by the shoulders, turned her and then gestured to one of the buffet tables, where a man stood talking to a server "—there he is."

Charlotte's mouth dropped open, and a wave of heat touched her from scalp to toes at the visceral memory of being draped over him. "How in the world—"

"Wait, you didn't invite him here?"

"Uh-uh."

"Then he—he *followed* you?"

"Why do you sound so freaked out?"

"Because guys who meet random women and then follow them without their knowledge are more often than not a little unhinged."

"Once a Fed, always a Fed." Charlotte patted Joey's arm, then turned again and kept the man in her sights. "I think I'll go over to see if you're right."

"I feel like there's a target on my back," Nate muttered to the server who stood at a buffet table pretending to arrange a silver tray of napkins that had been artfully folded into cranes.

"Don't." Vicky's white grin contrasted with her deep brown skin, and she was a refreshingly friendly face to see. At least the Blues had the sense not to jettison the catering company that had catered the Slayers' parties to perfection when the Francos had owned the team. "Dex

Harper was booted out. People will be too busy gossiping about him to notice there's a double agent among them."

"Double agent? How about a man who's just trying to keep his job?"

And get the team back under Franco ownership. It wasn't as if he hadn't been invited to the Slayers' party. What he *hadn't* been invited to do was dig around for any information that would help secure his spot on the team.

He had only one person to look out for: himself.

Nate whistled at the turnout. He'd give the new team owners credit: they sure as hell knew how to throw a classy party. What his father's fiancée, Bindi, wouldn't give to be on the guest list.

"Word is Dex lured two of the owners' daughters behind the stage. I wouldn't be surprised if he ends up with a broken kneecap for pulling that!"

Nate homed in on Marshall Blue. A cluster of tree-sized players surrounded him. Nearly hidden in the bunch was a slender woman whose body language screamed approachable and untouchable simultaneously.

"Not the GM," Vicky said. "She's been glued to her folks all night."

"Who's talking business?" He'd milled around, eavesdropped here and there, but hadn't overheard anything substantial.

"A couple guys from offense aren't looking forward to ice baths at camp. TreShawn Dibbs isn't so bulky this season, but that's just my observation," she said meaningfully.

Dibbs's contract with Las Vegas had sparked a firestorm several weeks ago, since no team wanted to touch him after his last season with the Chargers had ended with a row of suspensions topped with a steroid scandal.

"Oh," Vicky added, "the head coach was in a real private conversation with Blue's girl Charlotte, that trainer the hired. I couldn't glean much, though, since she snagged a carrot off my tray and sent me about my business."

On the drive over from the Rio, Nate had kept the satellite radio tuned to sports, regretting not catching up on Slayers news sooner. He'd caught snatches of reports sharing the same information—all three Blue daughters were somewhere on the team's payroll now.

And according to one blurb from the local sports-radio station, this Charlotte Blue woman was ready to get her hooks into the league's head-injury research.

His research. Hell, he had a right to take exception to a newcomer's plan to out-and-out bulldoze her way onto his family's team, into his work role and into the research— and probably the promotion—he was in line for.

If Nate could get his father to care about the franchise again, the man would realize that his formerly prized possession was drastically changing. Everyone was dispensable, including Nate.

Nate personally didn't care who formed the team so long as he or she knew what the hell they were doing. Not that his opinion was welcome to interlopers who had money to spend and power to spare.

"Vicky—"

"Shh! I need this job, so if anybody asks, you don't know me and I didn't tell you anything other than what's in the meatballs," Vicky muttered as she discreetly moved farther down the buffet table, straightening platters and bowls along the way.

A hand snaked up his arm, curved over his shoulder. "Nate?"

Be cool. Nate repeated it over and over in his head as he slowly turned. Was he going to be "booted" off the premises, too, just like Dex Harper? He leveled his gaze at the woman behind him.

Earlier he'd been ready to skip this party to be one-on-one with her. Then she'd walked out of his suite, leaving him on fire with want. Now she was close enough to kiss again and with that quirky smile was playing roulette with his restraint.

"Lottie."

"I—I can't believe you're here." A pause. "Um…*why* are you here?"

He could ask her the same question. Had she seen him get into his Benz and followed him here? But why go to the trouble? She'd been the one to shut down what he'd hoped would be a night of naughty acrobatics.

"Can't resist a good party," he said carefully. "You?"

"I couldn't have missed this even if I'd wanted to. Obligation and all that. Confused?" She went on after he brought his brows together in a frown. "See, this is *my* party. Well, my family and my team's."

Say what?

"Lottie," he said, his mind rushing to put it all together, knowing he wouldn't like what he came up with.

The female assistant athletic trainer whose name was all over the media, the woman who people called a jockette, was Charlotte Blue, the sexpot who not even two hours ago had been curled on top of him in his suite at the Rio… down to a silver scrap of underwear and a red bra.

Slayers colors.

Worse, the second he'd turned and recognized her, he'd wanted to touch her again. But back at the Rio she'd clearly prioritized her commitment to what he now knew was this team and her family over him. That much was clear. So he had to do the same and put himself and his agenda over the sizzle of desire that he knew logically was nothing but biology and physics and chemistry. And designed to drive a man out of his ever-loving mind.

"Charlotte Blue," he said, letting the syllables caress his tongue, "since we're doing the whole reality thing now, you should know I'm Nate Franco."

Suddenly she looked as shattered as he'd felt when she'd sashayed out of his suite.

And something about being the one to cause that expression to cross her face felt wrong.

Man, oh, man. This wasn't going to be easy.

But the line was drawn now, and they were on opposing sides.

Game on.

Chapter 4

A fling—make that a hot, brain-scrambling, unfinished one—wasn't supposed to be trouble. If done right. Charlotte had apparently made a misstep…because she'd lost control with Nate Franco. A teammate. The former owner's son.

A man who was the kind of trouble that would make an ordinary woman itch to be wrong. Charlotte couldn't afford this level of wrong. Nor could she find her voice even moments after Nate said, "You should know I'm Nate Franco."

He reached out as if to touch her sleeves. Instantly a sharp memory flashed of him tugging those sleeves until her dress slipped over her shoulders and down to the floor. Edging back before he could make contact, she said, "This is crazy."

"And not meant to be? You said that if it was meant to happen, we'd see one another again." Now he was tossing her words back to her, as if this were funny.

"That was before I realized you're on my team." At that, his gaze seemed to chill, and that hard look in his eyes was instantly familiar. She conjured an image of the man she'd glimpsed on ESPN. "Before I knew that you're Santino Franco's brother. I wasn't thinking. I lost track of—"

Nate shook his head, flattening his lips in contemplation. Private knowledge of what those lips could do sent a shiver through her. "No, Charlotte. You lost control. You liked it," he objected quietly, casually moving in closer. "I liked it."

"It was a mistake." And it wasn't fair that he could look so unruffled, cool and composed when she knew panic was written all over her. "Nate, we need to talk about this. It's no one's business but ours."

"A conversation between two people on my payroll is always my business," a man cut in.

Her father's voice was an injection of fear directly into her veins. He folded his hands over her shoulders and gave a little shake like when she'd been a child in need of care and consolation and all he could provide was a brisk shake and advice that she toughen up.

Charlotte watched Nate move his gaze from her to her father. Something in his face hardened for an instant.

Don't, she silently repeated. *Don't exploit the fact that I messed up.*

Nate glanced at her again and said to Marshall, "We were referring to the media. The employee roster, from the players to the front office, is the team's business, and not the media's."

If not for Marshall's steadying hands on her shoulders, Charlotte might have dropped to the floor in relief. But that strange look on Nate's face told her she wasn't completely out of the woods. They still needed that talk. Immediately.

"Damn right," Marshall said. "Glad you recognize that, Franco. Enjoy the party."

Clearly dismissed, Nate stepped away. Charlotte's eyes followed him until she blinked and lost him in the crowd.

"And you…" Marshall gave Charlotte a single firm clap between the shoulder blades "…don't look so nervous."

I chose the wrong man again, Pop. You and Ma were right. And if he talks, my career's as good as destroyed. Isn't that something to be nervous about?

When her father strode off, she searched the Bellagio's ballroom for Nate but had no luck in finding him again. That he could drop the bomb on her that he was on the training staff—that they were *colleagues!*—and then disappear from the party left her brain tangled and her heart in a panic.

Eventually her mother drew her aside. "Charlotte, is there something you haven't told us about your little discussion with Dex Harper earlier?"

Tem's voice may have been lullaby gentle, soothing, but it—and her face—were absent of anything but mild curiosity glazed with irritation. Concerned for her daughter she was not.

This time Charlotte was glad, because otherwise her parents would relentlessly dig until they got what they wanted. That was how they operated when it came to capturing something in their sights—information they wouldn't ordinarily be privy to…an NFL team that had solidly sat in the same man's possession since the establishment of the Las Vegas Slayers seventeen years ago… an impossible-to-get lakefront home that was currently being renovated and prepped for an HGTV *Million Dollar Rooms* segment.

Fortunately, no one but Joey had really witnessed Charlotte and Nate together—had seen the familiar way she'd curled her fingers around his shoulder, feeling solid muscle and the warmth of his skin beneath his shirt.

At least when Marshall had walked up on them, they hadn't been touching.

"Ma, if you want a moment-by-moment recap about the altercation with Dex, ask Martha. She was there, too."

"Interestingly, you and Martha have a history of coloring the truth. And not using the brains God gave you. You both should've called security on him straightaway."

"Have you told Martha this, or am I supposed to pass this life lesson along?" Charlotte ignored her mother's chilling look. "Well?"

Tem smoothed Charlotte's hair, grooming her not in a motherly gesture but only because she wasn't photo perfect in this moment. "I'd love to give your sister an earful about her irresponsible choices, but I can't find her."

Because Martha's smarter than you give her credit for. "Ma, please don't worry about Dex Harper."

"I'm worried about you. As your mother and your employer, I need to remind you that your place on this team is unique. You're a pioneer for women of color in professional sports now. I want you to treasure that and keep in mind that your decisions don't affect only you."

Charlotte never asked to be anyone's shining example—a part of her parents' "statement." She asked for a chance to prove her talents as a capable athletic trainer, but that hung in the balance all because she'd lost control with a man who'd now seemed to have vanished from the team's party.

"Everyone's watching, Charlotte. You can't risk making a mistake."

No kidding, she thought as Tem sauntered off, all poise and pride and perfection.

Charlotte was too gritty, too mistake prone, too real to truly be any of those things.

* * *

"Accidental sex with a coworker is impossible."

Charlotte's ballet flats scraped the pavement as she abruptly stopped in front of the entrance to the Forum Shops at Caesars Palace and discreetly glanced around to gauge whether any passersby had overheard Joey's declaration.

Muddled after realizing Nate's identity, she'd gone through the motions for the rest of last night and had lain awake through most of the early-morning hours until she could slip out of the villa for a hard run in scenic Mount Charleston without being subjected to a Blue-style inquisition.

But by the close of the night, when Charlotte, out of desperation to leave her family behind, had claimed fatigue, her sister Martha had zeroed in on her and lightly commented, "You say you're all tuckered out but you seem wide-awake to me."

At least Charlotte had effectively avoided Danica, the woman who was happily "the most stable of the Blue daughters"—until her recent split with a music mogul, that is—and now owned prime Las Vegas real estate thanks to her generous divorce settlement. This morning Danica had sent her a "What the hell?" text because they'd agreed to meet at Danica's place for a 5:00 a.m. eight-mile run together, and Charlotte had taken off at four. When afternoon had rolled around and Joey had called from her Bluetooth saying she'd left the Las Vegas field office for the day and was up for some shopping, Charlotte had leaped at the chance to vent about her latest Charlotte Slipup.

"Correction—it was almost-sex." Charlotte let her friend precede her into the crowded world of expensive upmarket finery. Over a hundred stores rolled out before her in gilded extravagance, and though she usually considered herself a marathon shopper, her zest for it had taken a hit. She was nervous—no, terrified—about repercussions. "Haven't *you* ever made a mistake like this? An office romance that was a *baaaad* idea?"

"Dozens," Joey admitted with a wanton little grin, pausing outside of Marc Jacobs. Still in her work outfit, a perfectly pressed dark pantsuit—and red-soled high heels—she appeared the picture of control and composure. But over the course of their friendship Charlotte had learned that Josephine de la Peña was a die-hard risk taker on and off the clock. "They were unwise, fun and *very* deliberate. Never accidental."

"Well, this one was."

"You didn't mean to go to his hotel suite for what was going to be full-blown S-E-X?"

Charlotte narrowed her eyes. "You can say the word, Jo. Just not so loudly that it ricochets off every statue in this place. Are we going in?" She gestured to the store's entrance.

"Nah, I'm moseying my way to Louis Vuitton and the Cheesecake Factory." Joey set off with her cane. "So, do enlighten me about this thing you call accidental almost-sex."

Charlotte struggled to put words to what she'd experienced with Nate before reality's invasion. It would be so easy to be swept away reliving everything from her first glimpse of him in her compact mirror to how close they'd stood without even touching on VooDoo's balcony to that first kiss in his suite. "Last night I didn't know how much I wanted to get away from myself—you know, the expectations and the pressure and the reporters and my family—until this man was in front of me, offering me a way out. I didn't know he was the old owner's son…Santino Franco's brother. God, he even looks like him." She snorted. "I got lost in wanting to do something I wasn't *supposed* to do."

"Boy, did you ever." Joey ambled to the base of a spiral staircase and rested her backside against the thick wall, easing the tension off her injured hip. She lifted her face, her gaze drifting up, up, up to the magnificently intricate ceiling. It was a wonder that many locals eventually took for granted. "Charlotte, perhaps he didn't follow you to the party, but…"

"What?" Charlotte waited until Joey met her eyes before she pressed, "Out with it, seriously. Don't try that 'protect her by keeping quiet' thing." Her college roommate, Krissy O'Claire, had chosen that route when she'd found out that Charlotte's then-boyfriend was a serial cheater, and after the truth finally erupted, Charlotte and Krissy had wound up going an entire semester without speaking. Charlotte didn't want to be "handled" again and needed her closest friends—Krissy and Joey—to never forget that.

"There are angles to this situation you're not really see-ing here, *amiga*," Joey said carefully. "The man was behind the bar at VooDoo, managed to say exactly the right things to get you off guard and then you did something 'acciden-tal.' Now you're in a situation that might have severe fall-out…because he's a Franco. Didn't Santino Franco—that tight end who got messed up early last season, right?—make a public statement suggesting your father threatened his father to get him to sell the team?"

Not *suggesting*. He'd outright accused, right after the transaction had been completed, but he hadn't followed up on the accusation, so there hadn't been further need for the Blues to defend themselves or go into damage-control mode. Her parents had made a singular response—that the sale was fair and final—and that had been the end of it.

Charlotte, figuring it was a nonissue, had turned her attention to other matters.

Like finding a way to be a part of her parents' most substantial acquisition.

"That was bogus, though, Joey. The owner himself never publicly said Pop bullied him, and yeah, Marshall 'The Body' Blue isn't a man anybody would be smart to mess with, but he doesn't bully to get his way. Plus, Santino hasn't said anything more about it."

"Not publicly, but can you be so sure he dropped his vendetta?" Joey gripped her cane with one hand and used the other to drum her French-manicured nails against her thigh. "Okay, follow me on this, Lottie, and let me talk. This is how I put things together."

An agent at work, Joey's expression drained of any humor and sunniness, her brows knit and she focused on a spot on the gleaming floor as people moved around them. Charlotte waited, pretty sure she had figured out the destination of her friend's train of thought.

"Your family's in the limelight, Lottie," she said quietly. "Your mother practically knows by name the paparazzi who follow her. Any Tom, Dick or Harry could've paid one of those buzzards to keep an eye on you. So you're being watched, all right, and opportunity knocks when you show up at the Rio after being put through the media wringer. Then *he's* there—Adonis, a gorgeous guy with beautiful skin and a cast-iron body who droves of women likely find attractive.

"Please don't look ashamed of yourself, Charlotte," Joey barreled on with a firm shake of her head. "You're not a fool. You're human. Hell, if I'd gotten to him first, I would've thrown my panties in the ring. But he wouldn't have wanted me…or anyone else at VooDoo. His endgame was to get under your armor, and where does that put him now? In prime position to exploit what happened between the two of you in his room. It may have been 'almost-sex' and it may have been accidental because you didn't know who he was. But what if he knew from the get-go who *you* were and what would happen if the two of you crossed the line?"

Charlotte hated every word of the speculation—every damn logical word of it. It had fallen too conveniently into place with Nate last night. If her phone hadn't beeped, if duty hadn't called, she wouldn't have left his suite until they were both spent and satisfied.

"Besides a scandal, what are the potential ramifications?" Joey asked.

"I don't exactly know. Suspension? Firing?"

Joey averted her eyes, chewing the inside of her cheek. She didn't bother protesting the idea that Charlotte's parents and sister would fire her, because she knew they would in a heartbeat.

"Nate would lose his job, too," Charlotte said, thinking out loud.

"His father sold the team. His brother doesn't play anymore. Maybe he's got nothing to lose, and damaging your credibility is worth it. Maybe hurting you is his way of giving the Blues something to remember the Francos by."

"I trusted myself with him," Charlotte said on a sigh. "I trusted a stranger."

"These hiccups happen, Lottie. I was on an undercover job a few years ago and opened myself up to a guy. He was black ops, didn't necessarily go by the same rules that I did. Long story short, he was playing me and he was dirty. It didn't end well, but what I got out of it was this. I don't trust strangers completely, but I always trust myself."

Charlotte nodded, and though she and Krissy from college were still close friends even as Krissy spent her sab-

batical from UNLV in California as a visiting facial plastic
surgeon, Charlotte was glad that Joey was the friend she
could lean on in this moment. Joey didn't normally go
deeper than vague when talking about her life as a DEA
agent. Charlotte always figured it had a lot to do with the
sensitive nature of her career, but clearly there was a level
of emotional distance Joey needed to maintain in order to
remain in such a dark line of work.

"What I've just unrolled for you is my theory, Lottie.
Find out if it's the truth. And in the meanwhile, how about
some Godiva chocolate cheesecake? I'll treat you, seeing
as you're going through all this and only got *almost-sex*
out of it."

A smile broke and Joey's throaty laughter was conta-
gious as she steadied her cane and took off walking again.
It went without saying that betrayal had tarnished Nate
Franco in Charlotte's eyes. Plus, there was bad blood between the Francos and the Blues, and Charlotte didn't want
to be a part of any drama that took her attention away
from football.

It was all about respecting and protecting the shield.
The landscape of the game was changing—the fact that
she even had a spot on the Las Vegas Slayers' training
staff attested to that. But at the core of it all, football was
a sacred sport.

To her, anyway.

Jeopardizing her career for a good time went against
her code.

"Hey, roadrunner." Danica's voice echoed off the high
ceilings and empty rooms of her *Architectural Digest*
three-story showcase home when Charlotte, weighed down
with shopping bags despite her intention to purchase only
a new charm for her Tiffany & Co. charm bracelet, let her-

self in sometime after sundown. "Next time you wanna bail on a run, give me a heads-up. I could've used that extra couple hours of sleep."

"Sorry, sorry, sorry." Charlotte kicked off her shoes, set her loot on the Crema Marfil marble floor and moseyed barefoot into the kitchen to see her sister had turned the room into a chef-style mini-office. Surrounded by folders and papers and pens and sticky notes, Danica sat at the island counter in jeans and a cutoff sweatshirt with her laptop in front of her.

As if thrilled to be interrupted, Danica pulled off her reading glasses, pinched the bridge of her nose and waved Charlotte over for a quick one-armed hug as if they hadn't just seen one another less than twenty-four hours ago. "Whaddup, sis."

"Hey." Charlotte lightly tugged her sister's flatironed ponytail. "Tough day?"

"Oh, your average contract drama. We've got a guy who's holding out. But it is what it is."

"Danica? I detest when people say that. What does that mean, it is what it is? It's the equivalent of the word *whatever,* only less succinct." As she spoke, Charlotte moved about the kitchen, sprinkling tap water into the pot of a sickly looking plant near the massive windows over the granite sink, putting out-of-place cooking utensils where they belonged, arranging pot holders and oven mitts.

"Lottie?" Danica offered a sweet grin. "I can't stand when people micromanage in my house."

"But it's a beautiful mess."

"*My* beautiful mess. That's the awesomeness of owning my own place."

Charlotte frowned, turning to her sister, who'd all but added, "You should try it yourself sometime." After bunking with Krissy in a college dorm for four years and renting a studio apartment in New England during grad school, she'd moved back home because there hadn't been a need to buy a place of her own once she'd started training college athletes in Nevada. Her parents had had plenty of room…and they'd insisted that she stay with them until she "got things together."

Danica had exchanged Marion Reeves's ring for a house key. Martha, on the other hand, had returned to her cozy childhood bedroom within a week of getting her hot little hands on her college diploma. She was a far cry from getting things together.

"Step away from the oven mitts, big sis."

"Fine. Whose pimped out Oldsmobile is that out front?"

"Marion's. He left his weight bench in the workout room, *had* to come for it tonight."

"This shouldn't be news to you," Charlotte said, picking up the remote to the small flat-screen mounted in one corner of the kitchen and selecting ESPN from the Favorites list, "but Marion has enough dough to own a few hauling companies of his own. Not to mention all the loyal fans who'd jump at the chance to help him move free of charge. My question for you? Why haven't you put a stop to this? Every time he 'remembers' that he left something behind, he ends up hanging out here for hours and staying for dinner and—"

"And nothing else," her sister interrupted emphatically. "We're not divorced with benefits. Make no mistake."

"Fine," Charlotte said again, though she wasn't completely convinced. But neither was Danica convinced that the division of marital assets was all that remained between her and her ex-husband, if the hesitation in her eyes and the nervous way she pushed her hair behind her ears was any indication.

"Why the impromptu sleepover?" Danica asked. "Finally sick of Martha's snoring?"

"No. I mean, of course I'm sick of our lovely baby sister's snoring, but that's not it. I could use some personal space."

"You'll get plenty of that here." Danica began shuffling folders in earnest, then muttered an expletive. "Matter of fact, it looks like I'll be taking off in a bit. Left something at the office. Don't bother waiting up."

Charlotte didn't care for the exhaustion and touch of loneliness in her sister's voice. She'd always figured Danica had gotten used to being defined as music god Marion Reeves's wife, and calling it quits to her marriage had forced her to accept someone she didn't yet know how to be: Danica Blue, a woman who deserved a life free of lies and mistrust and heartbreak.

Charlotte loved her sisters but didn't want what they'd gotten into—Danica's marriage, which apparently had more downs than ups, and Martha's gossip-fodder hard-partying lifestyle.

"Anything I can do to help?" Charlotte offered.

"Team-lift a weight bench," Marion cut in, swaggering into the kitchen in a silk shirt and designer slacks with a diamond buckle. The man was all about wearing his success. "You got the guns for it, Charlotte, so don't pretend you can't."

"Yes, I *can,* but I choose to instead put my feet up and watch your ass haul it out."

Marion rubbed a hand over his bald pate and scratched the back of his neck. "One of these days I'm going to win you over." Perhaps he thought he'd start by grinning that dimpled Mr. Personality grin that made his eyes crinkle at the corners—just one of his qualities that had roped Danica into a whirlwind relationship neither of them had been ready to commit to. At Charlotte's blank expression, he edged closer to Danica and peered over her shoulder.

"Buzz off. If you can't pull that bench out of here, I'm surrounded by muscle-bound men who're able and available."

"Quit tryin' to make me jealous. Aren't you seeing someone? What—he's not treating you right?"

"Ollie. He treated me much better than you did, and I still ended it." Danica blinked at him. "Weight bench?"

Marion squeezed her shoulder, but she didn't respond. "I'll come—"

"Come back for it," Charlotte and Danica finished in unison. Rolling her eyes, Charlotte stepped in, hoping her sister would forgive her for micromanaging this one last time. "Let me show you the way out, Marion."

"Nobody knows this house better than I do," he said, but walked with her anyway.

"Thought you wouldn't recognize it without all your Grammys and BET awards and NAACP—" Marion's shoulders stiffened and Charlotte stopped talking, resolving to give the man a break and walk him out without another word. It was difficult to remember that the man who'd cheated on her sister was still a person. For Charlotte, sometimes it was easier to forget that—easier to hold the grudge that truthfully wasn't her grudge to hold.

Shutting the massive door behind Marion, Charlotte returned to the kitchen with purpose. "Two things. Marion Reeves intended to lug a weight bench from the second floor in a *silk shirt*? And he also intended to haul away said bench in an Oldsmobile?"

Danica sighed, dragging a hand up her face and into her straight hair. "Didn't think about all that." She slid off the stool and gathered papers. "Oh, Charlotte, please don't start with me. When you've been married for a decade and suddenly you're not, it's tough to get used to it. Hopefully you won't ever experience that firsthand."

No, I probably won't. I can't even manage a successful one-night stand. Charlotte coughed at the thought. "Okay." Pitching in, she grabbed a stack of files and noticed one labeled Active Roster.

"Danica…you know what you said to Marion about being surrounded by available men? Well, that was just something you threw out there just to irk him, right?"

"Of course."

"So even if you wanted to pursue something—not implying at all that I think you do—could you?"

"What are you talking about?" Danica paused as she bent to retrieve her briefcase. "Pursue what? Like date one of our players or something?"

"A player, a coach, anyone."

Danica shot up. "Is that out there? Did anyone say I was dating someone from the team? Because I'm absolutely not. As the general manager I can't even fantasize about getting personal with someone I have professional power over. And the bigger problem—Ma and Pop would freak the f—"

"Thought so," Charlotte mumbled. But she wasn't the general manager, and her incident with Nate Franco had been a case of unknown identity. An honest mistake. Surely the front office and the league would understand that, if the details came tumbling forth? She and Nate knew exactly what had transpired—and Joey knew what Charlotte had told her.

Suppose everything were out in the open. Even if conflicted, Danica would simply do as their parents requested and fire Charlotte. Charlotte would love Danica for eternity, but nothing stood in her way of making their parents happy. It was what she did best.

If Marshall and Tem let it slide—which they most certainly would not—then media pressure, frequently an unstoppable force, would likely compel the league to interfere. Only in special circumstances did the National Football League grant a team true autonomy.

A sex scandal like this would only underscore the opposition's point that professional men's football was no place for a woman. The stance was sexist and in no way progressive, but clever-minded people had ways of twisting an honest mistake into a sordid scandal.

"Charlotte, why these questions? It's all a little random. What are you getting at?"

She barely heard her sister, preoccupied with the files in her hands. Did Danica keep a full employee roster on hand in her minioffice? Only one way to find out. Nonchalantly, she put the active roster file at the bottom of the stack she was holding and scanned the label of the next one.

"I'll take those," Danica said, her pitch a bit high as she reached for the stack. When Charlotte held on a moment longer than she should have, her sister yanked the folders away and snapped, "What are you doing?"

"Um…I was talking to someone at the party last night and have a question for him." She was dancing on thin ice now, telling sorta-truths to her sister, who had the power to fire her. "I didn't get his phone number."

Nate had *wanted* to exchange phone numbers, but she'd refused….

"This question of yours. Is it about business?"

"Absolutely." If Danica considered her older sister's career business. "I really need to get that number tonight— to ask him that question."

Danica went about packing her briefcase. Once finished she used the remote to click off the television and faced Charlotte. "A guy you were talking to at the party who

you *have* to ask a question tonight? Really, Charlotte?"
She sighed. "I know you asked Pop to introduce you to
Kip Claussen. He's married—"

The head coach? *Oh, noooooo.* "And stop right there.
Whatever you're thinking in that overly analytical brain
of yours, just stop. I don't want the HC's number."

"Then whose? Are you starting up something with a
team member? I really hope you're smarter than this."

"No, that's not what I'm doing." That was true—what
had started last night with Nate had also ended last night.
She just needed to make sure he knew that, too. "And what
wouldn't be smart? Me starting up with someone on the
team, or me disappointing Ma and Pop?"

"Both. So if I were you, I wouldn't consider doing either. Just sisterly advice." Danica grabbed the rest of her
paperwork and rushed upstairs to lock it away in her home
office, then hurried back to the kitchen. "Furthermore,
aside from a few folks I need to reach round the clock,
personnel contact information is stored securely at the
office. If you do have a strictly business question for this
man, ask him at training camp."

"Sure."

Car keys in hand, Danica reminded Charlotte what the
house's security code was and said, "Get in touch with
Martha if you want to call someone. Don't tell her I told
you—she wanted to break the news—but she said a journalist from *Sports Illustrated* is interested in scheduling
a chat with you."

Yesterday, before she'd let down her guard for passion,
Charlotte would've jumped for joy to catch the attention
of *Sports Illustrated.* Instead she felt as if she were holding her breath, waiting for Nate Franco to make a move
against her. If Joey's theory was correct—and her track

record in Las Vegas and D.C. said that she almost always was—then Charlotte had walked into a setup.

A worried look crossed Danica's face as she headed out. "I know how you've fought to get this far, Charlotte. Focus on that. Things are looking up for you."

And what went up came down.

Unless she could be an exception to the rule.

She needed to locate Nate Franco pronto, before training camp, and come to an understanding. Exposing what they'd done last night would benefit neither of them. Maybe Joey was wrong about Nate not having anything to lose....

Charlotte dug her tablet out of her handbag and settled on the big comfy family-room sectional. A Google Images search produced several photos of Nate Franco—mostly shots of him with his older brother, Santino. Side by side, the physical resemblance was shockingly clear. Aside from the fact that Santino was tattooed, wore his hair past his shoulders and had deeper creases in his face and a slightly crooked nose, he and Nate could be twins.

Nate had known just what to say to her, known to let her decide for herself whether she'd meet him at his suite or not. Known so very well where to touch her to make her mind melt.

Could something that had felt so dizzyingly natural really be false—a plot against her? Staring at a picture of the two brothers with an older couple, Joey's words found their way to her lips. "Were you playing me, Nate?" she whispered. She navigated the webpage to read the article that accompanied the photo. An Italian man and African-American woman—Alessandro and Gloria Franco. Nate's parents.

She found a crumb on the web trail that led her to where Nate was expected to be two evenings from now. The website for Young Minds, Bright Futures, a charity organization founded to provide scholarships to academically gifted children, listed Nate as one of the prominent people expected to be in attendance.

"Aren't you sick of me yet?" Joey greeted when she answered her phone, her dry humor a welcome familiarity.

"Quite the contrary," Charlotte said, putting the phone on speaker and rereading the online local events calendar. "How about I repay you for that yummy Godiva chocolate cheesecake with a pass to the Young Minds, Bright Futures fund-raising gala Thursday night. It's a charity function for academically gifted kids."

"Hmm. How *do* I feel about hanging with kids who are half my age—or younger—with bigger IQs than mine?"

"Nate is going to be there. And so am I. Danica refused to give me access to the employee roster, so I couldn't get his number."

"It would've been easier if you'd just asked me to get the dude's digits for you."

"Jo, none of that secret-agent snooping stuff, okay?"

Joey sighed, and Charlotte glanced toward the phone with a smile. "Why bring me along, then?"

"Hey, I said you couldn't snoop around in his background. I didn't say you couldn't observe. So what do you say? No matter, I'll be there and I *will* get answers."

She intended to get to Nate Franco before he did something they'd both regret.

Chapter 5

Already Nate regretted this. Coming off an early-morning sit-down with the Slayers' head trainer and a full day of prep at the team's training facility, Desert Luck Center, in Mount Charleston, he'd intended to close himself off to the world for the rest of the night, finalize plans for the Young Minds, Bright Futures fund-raiser tomorrow, put a thick steak on the grill, and review injury reports, progress notes and medical chart copies that had been released to him.

Then his brother had called, and Nate had changed course. Now his Benz shot through the city streets, blowing past blurs of vehicles and faceless motorists. Nightlife was in full swing—neon lights flashing, casinos bursting with gamblers, tourists and locals meshing on the Strip.

His destination lay deeper into the desert mountainside. As traffic thinned, he eased his foot off the gas pedal in spite of an intensifying mix of stress and anger that was encouraging him to stomp the accelerator in order to get

to his family's Lake Las Vegas estate—and *leave* again—
as speedily as his car could take him.

Calming down took some effort. The crisp jazzy music
coming from the car's radio helped. Leisurely now, he held
to the road's dips and curves until he reached the outer
edges of Vegas. Nestled in the Nevada mountains with the
lake in the background, his father's resort neighborhood
was a place of pristine palm-tree opulence. What people saw on the outside of Al Franco's multimillion-dollar
stately retreat—with its eight-car garage, which housed
his vintage-automobile collection, and its diverse array
of shrubbery, which reflected his fiancée's new hobby as
an amateur topiarist—was only a faint mirage compared
to what existed inside the twelve-thousand-square-foot
property.

For one thing, despite coexisting in a house spacious
enough to get lost in, Nate's brother and Al's fiancée
couldn't seem to avoid getting in each other's faces. Santino's girlfriend, a high-maintenance type like Bindi, had
dropped him for a New England Patriot less than a month
after his NFL career had snapped right along with one of
his spinal disks. Santino resented that Alessandro Franco
seemed intent on replacing his first wife with a trophy.

Nate knew his mother had been Al's goddess, his advi-
sor and friend, his conscience…his soul. Al had simply let
go of everything, including their two sons, when she died
three years ago. Their love had been the kind that when it
went away, it took his sanity, too.

Now Al was nothing more than prime media fodder.
The man who'd once been known for his need to win had
become a laughingstock, the very definition of a loser.
In two years he'd remarried and divorced twice. Both ex-
wives had been more interested in using his clout to build
their own celebrity and had ravaged his bank accounts dur-

ing the divorce proceedings, which had been quick but not painless. His current fiancée, Bindi, didn't appear to be any different and had been trying to get a cable network to roll out the red carpet for a reality television show about her life as the soon-to-be wife of an NFL team owner.

But Al had felt pressured to sell the team, Bindi was getting restless, the entire Franco bunch was out of whack and Nate was taking the heat.

Nate's interest was not just reclaiming ownership of the multimillion-dollar asset the Blues had stolen from the Francos for his brother, who'd saved his ass more times than Nate probably deserved. And it wasn't just about returning to his father what the aging man had built and what had mattered more to him than even his own children, though he'd never let anyone call him on that fact.

Nate was out to protect Nate. Framed diplomas for his degrees in kinesiology and sports medicine, certifications and that glorious PFATS award he'd been humbled to receive back when each new accomplishment was something to be treasured and not coolly tallied up like just another stepping-stone to ultimate success showed a man who looked good on paper but who walked in his brother's shadow. They didn't reveal all the close calls he'd faced growing up and how his brother—and luck—had helped him step out of one life to become the man he was today.

Every merit badge he'd earned—whether science-fair ribbon or medical fellowship or the NFL internship that had opened the door to professional sports training—was another piece of armor, shielding him from the sting of his unrealized dream of making his father proud. He'd gotten an education, all right, but all the hell he'd faced as a boy who was more nerd than jock had taught him how life, and the streets, worked.

Now the "science nerd with the silver spoon" was in

league with the same type of guys who'd tormented him back in the day, but they now respected him and depended on his elite set of skills for their professional and personal survival.

Now high-caliber women, who'd looked right through him back then, pursued him ferociously. Women like Bindi. And Charlotte.

Nate could go days without seeing Bindi. He had a place in Vegas and could book a suite virtually anywhere when the mood struck him if he wanted to disconnect himself from his family.

Common sense said Santino and Bindi ought not live together—even in a house that had more bedrooms than humans had fingers. When it came to stubbornness, they rivaled each other, and neither would concede to the other by moving out. Santino had taken it upon himself to keep a close watch on their father, and the only way to do it was to live with him. Now more than ever, Al needed family nearby.

And Al, in the center of it all, refused to intervene. When he wasn't out and about, making appearances, showing the world that losing three wives—one to death and two to divorce—and his NFL team hadn't broken him, he was locked in his rooms alone, showing only the people who truly knew him that all that loss *had* broken him.

So it was Nate's duty to step in, run interference, be the peacemaker whether he wanted to or not.

Ignoring Santino's call would've only put off the inevitable. He couldn't cut himself off from his family or dodge their demands. He could only do whatever he could to get them the only tonic that might cure them: the Slayers franchise.

The team was what had defined his father—the possession he'd treasured most. It was Santino's birthright, which he'd wanted to operate down the line, and his connection to it had been the only light in his world after his injury and his girlfriend's betrayal. And as for Bindi, the woman swore up and down that she could be a wonderful wife to Al but she'd never been shy about wanting the team back so that she could move forward with her reality TV idea. There could be no show about her life as an NFL team owner's fiancée/wife, because her fiancé no longer owned an NFL team.

Instead, Al had given up his team for a generous fortune that he appeared to be just sitting on. No investments, no purchases…and even Bindi hadn't gotten more trinkets or pampering out of the transaction.

Nate never understood how Al could sell the team without consulting with his heirs, especially now that the man still hadn't any plans of what to do with the proceeds.

It only made sense that he'd been coerced into the deal, that the team had been muscled away from him through threats to hurt him and the people close to him. That was what Al had told Santino and Nate when they'd first realized the sale was happening, but even when Santino barged ahead ready to fight, Al hadn't wanted to talk. Out of pride, out of fear, it didn't really matter to Nate.

Corporate bullies were no different than thugs on the street. Nate had had run-ins with both.

Which was why he could handle Marshall Blue.

But can you handle his daughter Charlotte?

Nate shut off the engine and let his gaze sweep the premises of his father's estate but saw only a vision of Lottie—*Charlotte*—bared to him in red-and-silver lace and chocolate diamonds.

Cutting things short with her in his hotel suite had been torture but maybe a good thing after all. She hadn't gone running to Daddy and Mama to order him off the team.

He hadn't seen her at the training facility today, which was perfectly reasonable since camp hadn't officially begun yet, but no one he had encountered today had given any indication of knowledge that he'd crossed a line with the big boss's daughter.

Could be she wouldn't talk. Or she was biding her time?

With a fresh wave of frustration falling over him, Nate strode up to the door and was greeted by the housekeeper, Nadia, whose pinched expression spoke volumes about the storm brewing inside, which he could hear from the doorstep.

Nate took a fortifying breath and jammed his hands into his pants pockets, moving unhurriedly behind Nadia to a living room the size of a small stadium. Surrounded by Asian-inspired decor were Bindi and his brother, yelling across the room at one another.

At the sight of Nate, Bindi, in her tight-as-a-glove dress and pearls, with her blond hair twisted neatly, scoffed and brought a wineglass to her lips, retreating to the corner opposite to where Santino stood leaning heavily on the baby grand piano with his hands curled into fists and his face weary. They were like boxers waiting anxiously for the next round to begin.

"Can't you fight your own battles?" Bindi said to Santino, ignoring Nate. "Why bring your *little brother* into this when it has zilch to do with him?"

Nate kept his expression mild, exchanging a look with Nadia as she slipped away from the action. At six-four he was two inches taller than his brother and not quite as compact. Those who didn't know Nate and Santino had to look hard to find their differences and guess which was the elder brother.

Both were older in age and experience than Bindi Paxton, who at twenty-nine had been sheltered in a rich girl's world until her parents had cut her off for behavior that had reflected poorly on her father, a disgraced congressman.

"A producer was here, from some cable network," Santino told Nate, pulling out the piano bench and lowering onto it.

"He was *my guest!* You had no right to throw him out," Bindi said. "When we get the team back, I want to redecorate for the show. Some of the filming will take place here."

"You never had any claim on the Slayers," Nate clarified, striding farther into the room, drawing her full attention now. "That needs to always be clear. It's my father's team. Santino and I are in line—not you."

"It's not my team anymore."

The three of them turned to see Al in the entryway. His well-cut designer suit couldn't disguise how truly unwell he was—his gray hair was mussed, his eyes sunken and hollow, and his face gaunt.

"I'm sorry about that." This he said to Santino, as he walked over to clasp his shoulder. "It's gutting you, and I didn't want that, but it is what it is."

God, how Nate hated that phrase. He watched his father clap Santino's shoulder, watched him apologize with words that wouldn't help the situation but also with heartfelt sincerity.

And none of that sincerity was directed at Nate.

Out the corner of his eye, Nate watched Bindi lower her wineglass and turn slightly toward him with her lips parted in surprise. As if she'd just seen him from a new vantage point.

"What if you did get the team back, Dad?" Nate asked. "You said you didn't want to sell but had to because Marshall Blue threatened to have someone come after you."

"Getting it back is impossible," Al replied, averting his eyes. The thing Nate had respected about his father the

most—his ability to always look someone in the eye—
was gone.

"What if it's not—"

"I said impossible. Damn it, Nate. Can you leave this
alone? All of you. Leave it alone." With that, Al started
out of the living room, but Bindi stopped him, striding
with purpose in her stylish dress and high heels that were
made more for fashion than function.

"Alessandro, I won't let you give up. Now stop wallow-
ing and let's go out. Or, better yet, let's stay in and discuss
a wedding date, because planning ahead is the best—"

He shook off her touch, growling, "Go a month without embarrassing me on some gossip site and maybe then
we can talk dates."

Santino's posture straightened and Nate looked over
in time to see Bindi step back, struck by Al's words. Un-
characteristically, this time she didn't egg him on but gave
him the space he needed to stomp out of the living room
and probably into the home theater or his private rooms.

"He's unhappy," Bindi said, blinking her crystal-blue
eyes.

"Pushing him into a walk down the aisle won't make
him happy," Nate replied. Though his father's insult was
uncalled for, Bindi needed to ease up…and come to the
conclusion that Al Franco wasn't the man for her.

Nate and Santino had been trying for months to convince their father to call off the engagement. It was possible that Al genuinely cared for Bindi, and vice versa, but
Nate wasn't banking on it. What he did know about their
relationship disgusted him: Al had proposed to Bindi because she was withholding sex—holding out for a signed,
legal marriage license. Al was drawn in by her attrac-
tiveness, charm and penchant for sexy clothes. She was a
challenge. But not once had he told her that he loved her.

To some people love didn't matter, and Bindi wasn't likely going to let her youth slip away waiting for it to come along.

"Fine. I'm going out. But don't worry—I'll be back." Bindi set her wineglass down hard on the nearest table and seemed satisfied when droplets of the liquid sloshed onto the wooden surface. "Boys, it's been real."

Nate waited until Bindi had left the room before he went after his father.

"Dad—"

"Let it go, Nate."

"I can't. The Blues didn't take the team away from only you. They took something that belongs to Santino and me. Didn't you think about your sons when you were signing those papers?"

"I had no choice." Still, Al couldn't look him in the eye.

"Telling Santino, telling me, was always a choice. We're invested in the team, too. You were going to put him in control of operations. That was the plan. For the Slayers to stay in the Franco family." Nate reined in his frustration, gentled his tone. "Dad, you weren't the kind of man who'd give in to anyone's threats. And you used to give a damn about the team's stats. For two seasons the Slayers failed to make it to play-offs, and not once did you make any personnel changes."

"Don't you criticize my judgment. I had the franchise for seventeen years."

"It crashed and burned the last two of those years. And now it's out of our hands."

"That's how it's going to stay, Nate."

"What about your fiancée? She wants it back." At Al's warning glare Nate pressed on. "If she's with you only to get a TV show, and you're with her only to get into her pants, then you both should cut your losses. Marriage isn't the answer."

"You and Santino don't get to tell me what to do. Let *me* handle Bindi and my team."

"It's not yours anymore," Nate said quietly.

"That's right, son." Al tapped a finger to the center of Nate's chest. "Remember that."

Nate watched Al stride off. Then he returned to the living room, weighed down with defeat.

"Get anywhere with Dad?" his brother asked.

"Nah. Reversing the sale would be easier if Dad would just report to the league that he was coerced into selling the team. It's like trying to help someone who doesn't want to be helped."

"Can't think that way, bro," Santino said, his face stony. "*I* need this, too. I've got nothing else—no career…nothing."

"I get that, man. But what about that analyst gig?" Almost immediately after his retirement had been announced, ESPN reps had started courting him.

"It's not the same as being on that field, in the game. Nate, I never asked you for anything growing up, but I can't do this without you. You're on the inside."

For now, just as Bindi said.

"I heard about the new assistant trainer, the daughter—Charlotte Blue. You've met her by now, right?" When Nate nodded, he went on, "Get a feel for what she's about?"

Nate got a *very* thorough feel on Charlotte—how her hair felt between his fingers, how her mouth tasted, how her thigh muscles tightened when he touched her intimately—but he didn't know what her motives were.

"Not yet," he told his brother. "But I will."

"Then I can count on you to get this done?"

Santino had saved Nate's life, had yanked him off the

path that would've led right to Nate ending up a tragic sta-
tistic. His brother had restored his future. It was time Nate
returned the favor.

"By any means necessary."

Enveloped in leather and polished wood, in the vintage glory of the Hard Rock's renovated Body English
bar, Bindi Paxton let the gray-haired man at the end of
the bar put her liquor on his tab. As the bartender placed
another whiskey sour and a fresh napkin in front of her,
she moved her gaze past the handful of other patrons over
to her benefactor.

He wore a charcoal-colored suit. Judging by the exquisite styling, she doubted it cost anything less than a
few grand. His hair was perfectly groomed, his face was
smooth-shaven, and his eyes were fastened on the drink
in his hand. She registered that he wore a wedding band,
then moved on to something more interesting—the contents of his glass. It was his third single-malt whiskey. He
thought he had sought her out, but she'd had her eye on
him since he strode up to the bar.

Ever since her parents had turned her loose with no
financial cushion, she'd learned to be observant when it
came to men. It was all part of survival.

Bindi crooked a finger at the bartender, leaned forward and added a smile. "Can I count on you to keep my
drinks coming?"

"Sure you can handle more whiskey?" The words were
skeptically spoken.

"I wouldn't ask for more if I wasn't sure." She swiveled around on her stool, crossed one long leg over the
other and surveyed the room. The golden overhead lights
were dim, but the sparkling chandeliers gave it a subtle
radiance. The bar's mostly well-dressed patrons gathered

around the tables or in booths, while others crowded the bar, tossing back wine and hard liquor.

In her opinion, a hotel lounge wasn't the epitome of a classy social scene. She preferred mingling at country clubs and had a special love for Cleopatra's Barge. Up until a few months ago she'd even loved sharing the finest wines and dirtiest gossip with her girlfriends in the Wine Society.

One flop of an engagement had severed her valuable connections, but she was determined to bounce back. She hadn't gotten where she was today, driving a Lamborghini and jet-setting in Manolo Blahnik heels, by setting limits for herself.

Running her finger over the rim of her glass, she eyed the exec as he made his way over to her. Conversation and subdued laughter surrounded them. She set her glass aside, pointing to his hand. His wedding band had vanished. "Put it back on," she said.

A puzzled look played over his face. "Excuse me?"

"Put the wedding ring on your finger." Once he obeyed, she slid off the stool.

"I'm Leonard."

"Now tell me what you're about before I get bored."

Leonard followed her to one of the leather booths. "Your friend Toya Messa told me you have a problem."

What'd you know? There *were* some loyal friends in this town. "My future's down the toilet. Got a plunger?"

"Not quite. I do have access to sensitive information—off-the-books sort of stuff—that people would kill for."

"Funny."

Except Leonard didn't crack a smile.

"Well, what can you do for me?"

"That depends on you."

Bindi smoothed her hair, though she knew it was perfectly twisted with not a strand out of place. This was getting complicated. All she wanted was what Alessandro Franco had promised her when he'd told her she was gorgeous and had given her the diamond ring she twisted around her finger now. They'd met at a bar much like this one. He'd been down in the dumps and she'd let him talk it out. He'd also wanted sex—most men who pursued her did. But she'd been smart about it this time. By denying him, she'd gotten an engagement and would eventually get the security of a prenup-free marriage.

She hadn't risen to these heights to be dropped on her butt. A blink ago Vegas had been Al's throne, and she'd been at his side. The new queen. She didn't have to lull herself to sleep with delusions, didn't have to live every waking moment with fear riding her. A producer had noticed her. She was going to get her piece of the reality TV pie—her own cable show.

She had money and a man.

Now she had a glass of whiskey that had come up empty without her realizing it.

"Just pay the tab and give the bartender a nice big tip, and we'll talk," she said to Leonard, reaching for her phone. "Let me discuss this with a friend."

"Are we getting someone else involved?" A muscle twitched in his face. Annoyance.

"He needs saving as much as I do," she said. Last night at Al's house Nate had been slighted, overlooked by his father. Bindi had noticed Al favored Santino, and she knew Nate realized it, too. He wasn't quite as jaded as his brother, and she was grateful for that. He didn't know it yet, but they were destined to be allies, to work together to get Al's team back under his control.

Bindi didn't believe for a second that the man who'd sworn to protect her and make her happy would willingly give up his fortune to a pair of strangers. Of course Marshall Blue had forced his hand!

Well, soon enough he'd be sorry that he had.

Bindi waited until Leonard walked off to the bar before she dialed Nate's number.

Predictably, the call went to voice mail. Nate didn't answer her calls and only sporadically returned her texts. She kept the message short but urgent.

"While I was at the bar, paying for your drinks, I started thinking," Leonard said, coming up behind her. Too close for her comfort. "In this economy, getting your money's worth really is all that matters."

"Really." Bindi knew she wasn't going anywhere—unless it was out of the Hard Rock Hotel—alone. Though she withheld sex from Al, she'd never cheated on him and wouldn't start today, especially now that their engagement was hanging on by a thread as fragile as a spiderweb.

"What if I got us a room and we settle up there?" Leonard suggested.

"Go up and wait for me." *And hold your breath while you're at it!*

Leonard left Body English fast, and Bindi could think again. She was supposed to be done with sleaze and schemes, but just when she thought she was over the past, some new twist was there to pull her back again. Wasn't that the thing about life? People thought they were moving along, changing, growing, going forward, but it was made up of circles.

Finally Al's son appeared at her booth. "What's the emergency?"

"My marriage. And your job." When he mumbled a curse and turned to leave, she snagged his hand. "Sit down. Please quit pretending you're not as self-absorbed as I am."

Nate freed his hand but sat. "What is it, Bindi?"

"The Slayers belong to Al. He said he didn't want to sell."

"I know that."

"So we're going to get the team back for him."

"There's never been a 'we,' Bindi, and there never will be."

Under all that cockiness was the same desperation she saw in the mirror at the end of the day when her face was vulnerable without makeup. It was a sad thing to live without security. She'd had enough of that after her parents cut her off. He was living through practically the same uncertainty now, not sure how long he'd even be on the Slayers' payroll. She sort of felt sorry for him but sorrier for herself.

"United or not, we need the team back in your father's name. Santino needs it, too."

"Santino thinks this is none of your business."

"Well," she shot back, holding up her ring, "this says that it is."

"I'm not going to raise hell at camp, if that's what you're hoping."

Hell-raising wouldn't be effective, not when he was probably two seconds from being dumped off the team's training staff anyway. "You're at risk. Charlotte Blue is after something. A girl can tell when another girl is after something. What if she has her eye on that head-trainer position you were talking about?"

Nate's face was like granite. She'd struck the nerve she'd been looking for.

"I know someone who can help us take care of this. All he's going to do is a little careful digging. It's about knowledge, that's all. What makes Charlotte Blue a better fit for that head-trainer job than you? What makes Marshall and Temperance Blue think they can force a man to sell his franchise? The news and everyone else is calling it the 'Blue Dynasty,' as if the team's been reborn or something." She leaned forward. "A woman like Charlotte has dirt in her past, I know it. Help me help you, Nate."

Was that conflict in his eyes? No, just a trick of the vintage chandelier lighting. "What do you want me to do?"

"Trust me to get this taken care of." Forget Leonard. She could restore Al's team and her life without the meddling of some slimy P.I. her friend Toya had probably found in the Yellow Pages.

Nate's laugh was ironic. "I'll never trust you, Bindi."

Fortunately, there was never any honor among thieves… or liars and manipulators. "No prob. All you need to do is cooperate."

Chapter 6

Appealing to a man's humanity was a delicate task, especially when the man was one who'd seen you in your Skivvies and possibly had a score to settle. Nate Franco's grudge was sorely misdirected if it included Charlotte. She would make him see that. Tenacious, persistent, relentless. Those qualities were waiting to be unleashed, and tonight she was ready to approach the complicated situation with Nate from whatever angle necessary to convince him to keep what happened privately between them *private*.

Dressed for the occasion in a black tiered Dior dress, haute stockings and boa stilettos—plus the one thing she felt naked leaving the house without: confidence—she set the Taccia fountain pen on the bid sheet for the one-carat musgravite sheltered in a lighted display case, cast a final look at the gemstone with every intention of circling back as the silent auction drew to a close and moved outside to observe the guests roaming the JW Marriott's Valencia Terrace.

No sign of Nate. She'd kept watch for him in the ballroom while viewing the high-ticket merchandise and services that had been donated to the Young Minds, Bright Futures scholarship ceremony and charity fund-raiser. Surely he would be here to at least congratulate the highest bidder of the pair of tour passes to Slayers Stadium, which included tickets to the bidder's choice of any one home game. Good seats, too, on the fifty. Likely the donation had been promised to the fund-raiser before the Blues had acquired the team, and Charlotte appreciated that it hadn't been retracted.

But Nate was absent from the room that was flooded with children and teens of varying ages—some withdrawn and overwhelmed by the linen-and-golden-light splendor that was all in their honor, others charged with excitement and thriving off the rush of being the center of attention.

Behind the podium was a well-guarded table that held gold-lettered plaques and gift certificates for the scholarship recipients, paid for with the year-round contributions from the event's sponsors and generous benefactors. For every child in attendance there seemed to be at least three adults present. Among the sea of people were parents and guardians, social workers and teachers, waitstaff carrying platters of appetizers and kid-friendly beverages, as well as the occasional city official, journalist or celebrity.

A blueberry mojito in hand, Charlotte surveyed the ebb and flow of guests on the terrace, searching for a man with a burr haircut and dark eyes that had seemed to hold the power to look right through to her every unspoken wish. What would be his motive for not showing up to this fundraising event, when the announcement she'd found online had all but gushed over his generosity and dedication to children's literacy and academic excellence?

Had he guessed she would attempt to find him here and backed out of the commitment? Not only did the sneakiness of the move frustrate her, but Charlotte found it intolerable that he'd brush off an event and cause he was supposedly so devoted to.

Or his absence could have nothing at all to do with her.

Why do I care one way or another? Why am I even hoping he's a better person than that?

Charlotte returned her attention to the mojito and let a circle of women draw her into a conversation about the benefit.

Yesterday she'd contacted the event's chairperson and made an anonymous donation to the Young Minds, Bright Futures charity. She approved of the cause that offered Clark County's academically gifted children the recognition they deserved no matter their families' incomes or social statuses. While some of the silent-auction items offered entertainment, many were scientific in nature—such as the gemstone Charlotte had her eye on—and the proceeds from all would be funneled into the charity's scholarship fund.

She'd come here for one mission, but in between searching for Nate she found herself enjoying the atmosphere and the company of brilliant, humble kids and the grown-ups who were not only present to share the glory but appeared genuinely proud.

In that respect they were more fortunate than Charlotte had ever been.

As the conversation waned and a few of the women stepped away, Charlotte finished her mojito and found Joey leaning back against a wall at the opposite end of the terrace, clad in leather pants and a hunter-green Naeem Khan peasant blouse. "I don't think Nate's going to show," Charlotte said. "And I was so looking forward to playing spy."

"I found out that Nate participates in this benefit every year. It hits close to home for him, turns out. He's a brainiac, too." Joey hitched her chin up at the sun bleeding hues of orange and purple into the horizon. "It's early. He'll probably show. Are you going to take off?"

Charlotte preferred to stick around for the ceremony and the results of the silent auction, but the idea of Nate turning his back on these kids and this fund-raising event—to avoid her?—left her feeling unsettled. The fact that it bothered her was even more troubling.

"Maybe," was her uncertain answer. "For a woman who wasn't too enthusiastic about making an appearance here, you sure seem comfortable," Charlotte noticed, realizing for the first time that Joey held two glasses. And both contained what looked like tropical punch garnished with orange slices.

Joey's gaze lowered slightly as she sipped from the glass with the lipstick-stained rim. "I met a cop. His name's Parker."

"That's great!"

"He's a widower. Has a son." Joey held up the second glass in explanation. "An actor from that FX show about a motorcycle club is here, and Parker took his kid to get an autograph." She polished off her juice and handed Charlotte the glass, then straightened and grabbed her cane from its hiding spot behind her.

"You hid your cane?" Charlotte whispered. "If you like this cop so much that you're holding his son's juice glass, you should find out up front if he has a problem with your injury."

"Lottie, it's not like I looked at him and saw wedding bells. I guess I was pretending for a bit that I'm one hundred percent whole…. Dumb." She laughed, but it lacked warmth or humor. "Anyway, I didn't come here to find a guy. I came to help you scope out Nate."

"Things have an odd way of changing course sometimes," Charlotte said, but she'd let her friend make her own choice. She handed Joey's glass to a waiter and turned discreetly, scanning faces. "Which one's Parker?"

Now Joey's smile was authentic, and she braced her weight on the cane, carefully taking inventory of the terrace crowd. "Over there by the band. Dark hair. Dimples. Roman nose… Isn't that what they call it?"

The man bent to say something to the boy in front of him, and both women fell silent, enjoying the view.

"Somebody's got a crush," Charlotte whispered.

"He's a *dad*. And his son's a ten-year-old physics genius, turns out."

"He's a man—" Charlotte paused as the man and his son turned to wave Joey over "—and both he and his kid seem taken with you. Get to know him, if you want a friend's suggestion."

Joey frowned, as if ready to protest, when something trapped her attention. She subtly lifted her brows at Charlotte. "Well. Here comes your man."

Charlotte felt Nate's approach even before she turned to see him backlit by the million dots of glowing gold from the lights that had been strung about the terrace. She thought she'd memorized every detail—his height, his bronze skin, that beautiful curve of his mouth—but seeing him weave through the clumps of guests, in an almost black suit and stark white shirt with no tie and an unbuttoned collar, jump-started her senses.

Something about him affected her in a way she couldn't define and certainly didn't want to accept. It was as if he'd figured her out even before meeting her. Without touching her, speaking to her or even looking at her, he called to her.

And this was how it had happened to begin with.... Except there would be no fantasies tonight. Just reality. Just business.

"I won't be far," Joey let her know in a low tone only Charlotte could hear before she slipped into the crowd.

Nate let his eyes touch her in one smooth stroke from her hair, which she'd wrangled into a high knot, to her boa stilettos. If he was waiting for her to react, he could keep waiting, because she wouldn't shrink or flush under his stare. Establishing right now that he didn't outmatch her was paramount.

"Funny how you and I never ran in the same social circles before you were hired," Nate said, his baritone tight with tension. He acknowledged a trickle of passing acquaintances—men in suits and women in soiree dresses—with easygoing nods and brisk handshakes before zeroing in on her again. "Is your interest in providing for incredibly studious kids new?"

Charlotte let the fire glint in her eyes but blinked it smoothly away after a moment. "I support this charity's mission and am glad the Las Vegas Slayers chipped in. But I'm here because I looked you up on Google and I need a word with you. In private."

Nothing like blunt honesty to throw a man off his game. She liked seeing surprise flare in his eyes but didn't bask in the satisfaction. Divulging the location of an unlocked meeting room that she'd found earlier, she instructed, "I'm going there now, but you'll need to wait some minutes before slipping out of the ballroom—"

"This feels familiar."

"I'll be a saint." Charlotte's mouth softened as if on the

verge of a smile, just enough to reel in his attention. "History won't repeat itself. I can promise you that."

She made haste, pretending to be on a pressing cell phone call as she walked with purpose through the halls, then dropping the phone into her tiny handbag when she found the vacant meeting room without anyone in her way or on her trail.

While she waited, she let her foot shake freely, getting the nervousness out of her system. It made no sense that he could rattle her so, when she'd come to this benefit to rattle him enough to drop whatever unfounded vendetta he had against her family.

If, in fact, he *had* one.

"The presentations will be starting soon," Nate said, coming into the meeting room that suddenly felt too small for the two of them, "so we may have to cut this short."

Charlotte let the razor-thin sarcasm pass but was stunned at Nate's audacity to set her up *and* be sullen about not finishing the job in his suite at the Rio. "Won't take long."

"What about your friend? Is she around or did she outfit you in a wire or something?" He must've noted the concern sweeping across her face, because he continued, "I saw her at the team party and again here, speaking with you. And she looks on edge, like she wouldn't trust a nun."

"My friend is here for moral support." *And to help me spy on you, of course.*

"Then a wire…?" Nate came farther into the room, into her space, and circled her, his gaze coasting deliberately, agonizingly meticulously over her every line and curve.

"That would be unnecessary, seeing as I came here only for a colleague-to-colleague conversation." Charlotte needed him to stop moving, to stop allowing his scent to wash over her and drag her memories back to dangerous moments. "I want to know if you set me up the other night at the Rio."

Nate did stop, as if frozen in place. "How would I have done that?"

She wanted to be able to see the truth in his eyes, to see deeply into him the way he'd seemed to be able to stare right to the core of her when they were just random strangers in a hotel nightclub. Or perhaps she hadn't been random to him but the woman he was after from the start. "Carefully but easily. You had someone follow me around and let you know where I was. Then you…pounced."

"Understand this. I didn't know who you were when we met. And it was all up to you, Charlotte. You came and went on your own terms. And why would I go to such lengths for sex?"

Oh, he wasn't going to throw her off with that. "Maybe sex wasn't your actual objective." Charlotte refused to look away, wouldn't let her nerves get the best of her. "Was sleeping with me going to be a bonus or a token or something?"

"No." The word was low, but it resounded in Charlotte's ears until it penetrated all the way down to her heart.

"Then what was your agenda…Nate Franco?" At his hesitation, she prodded, "Just admit that you have a problem with my family and with me being on the training staff."

"Damn right I have a problem with your family taking what doesn't belong to you." The truth ignited the heat in his eyes, and though the reality of it stung, Charlotte would've respected him less if he'd lied.

"Your father sold the franchise to my father. It was a fair deal."

"Preying on a man still grieving the death of his wife isn't fair where I come from." Nate pulled a chair back from the conference table and sat, watching her openly. He legitimately believed that her father had intimidated his father into selling the Slayers. It was absurd, because she knew it wasn't true. But to him…

"The Blues don't roll like that, Nate."

Whether he trusted what she told him or not didn't matter. She would help her parents fight whatever trouble the Francos sent their way…if they let her. Of course, if Nate decided to disclose the details of their first meeting, there was an almost certain chance that her parents would want her as far away from the organization as possible.

"What do you intend to do?" she asked, going to stand in front of him. "Notify my family and the media and the league that you saw Charlotte Blue's underpants? Is that the satisfaction you want?"

"What would that accomplish?"

"Nate, for starters it would get me off your territory. I'd be off the team." The possibility of losing it all hadn't felt quite as real as it did once she'd said the words to him aloud. "But so would you. Are you really so confident you can break down my family that you're willing to risk your own career?"

"Your family controls the front office. You're golden, Charlotte. As good as tenured on the damn training staff."

"Actually," she said quietly, "you have that 'family takes care of family' luxury. I don't. People on the outside calling foul, claiming nepotism? They're so wrong. None of you know my parents."

"Charlotte. You say my family takes care of one another."

"Clearly."

"Who takes care of you?"

I do. It's what I'm used to. But she wouldn't tell this man that. Already she'd said too much, let the conversation go too deep into waters she didn't want to disturb. He knew that he could hurt her…but would he?

Rather than press for an answer to his question, he came back with another one, getting to his feet as he spoke. "Who's to say *you* didn't plan to casually run into me at VooDoo?"

"Like I said earlier, the Blues don't roll like that. We play fair and that makes winning sweeter."

"You didn't know who I was?" he countered.

"I didn't realize you were Santino Franco's brother until you told me your name at the party."

"Santino's brother." A rueful smile touched his face. "Yeah, he was the star. I was a competent athlete but didn't have the same 'star quality,' so I hung somewhere in the background…a nerd…a kid who was all about the books, just like the kids being honored in this building tonight."

So he *was* committed to the charity's cause. Did he see aspects of his younger self in the kids in the Valencia, kids who were gifted in some ways but disadvantaged in others?

"No one should be overlooked or forgotten."

Was he referring to the kids who now had "bright futures" or himself…or her?

Charlotte hadn't realized that with each sentence he'd come a step closer to her, and now he was in her space again.

"After this, you'll remember *me*." Nate tucked her against the wall of his body and fit his mouth over hers.

At his impassioned touch, Charlotte felt herself going willingly deeper down the path that had put her square in the middle of this mess in the first place, but the last thing she wanted to do was disengage from a man who was talking to her—not with words but with lips and tongue.

His hands found their way between them, roaming over her from breasts to belly, then found their way around to her rear. All the while his mouth was hot and dangerous and *so* thorough.

When he finally released her, she staggered, momentarily dazed, and for a long moment there was only the ragged sounds of their breathing.

Charlotte smoothed her dress. "Told you I wasn't wearing a wire."

"Had to know what you intended to do," he said, volleying her words back to her, his voice rough like gravel.

"I intend to go to Mount Charleston and do my job." She headed for the door.

"Charlotte...I won't take any cheap shot against you. But the one thing worse than getting hot with you when I didn't know you were my coworker, that you're a Blue, would be to get hot with you again."

"Then don't do it." She rolled her tongue over her bottom lip and could taste him there. "See you at camp."

Desert Luck Center, the Las Vegas Slayers' training facility, spread out over a corner of Mount Charleston, Nevada, was architectural heaven, with its most grand outdoor features being two practice fields, a basketball court and an Olympic-sized swimming pool. Beyond the spacious lobby, the sprawling main building housed a weight room, equipment room, cafeteria, auditorium and lounges for players and staff.

Like the first day of school, Charlotte thought as she parked her Fiat in the lot, hitched the strap of her duffel bag over her shoulder and hurried inside out of the light summer drizzle. Growing up, she'd been that oddball girl who was excited at the start of a brand-new year but who purposely wore the previous year's clothes just because everyone else would be decked out in brand-new stuff, making every classroom smell like a department store.

Today, though, brand-new athletic shorts peeked out from underneath her favorite oversize cotton T-shirt.

Today she was more anxious than excited. It was imperative that she check her nerves at the door and present a cool exterior. If she could show up to camp every morning and return to her temporary "villa home" each afternoon knowing that her presence on the staff had made a difference, then she'd be all right.

She'd expected uncomfortable glances from players and coaches alike but had not expected to locate her assigned locker and see a new-with-tags push-up bra taped to the door.

A few muffled snickers rode the air.

Wasn't this supposed to be *professional* football? Even her college athletes and colleagues hadn't stooped low enough to pull this kind of junior high prank. She peeled the garment away and twirled it around her finger. "Oopsie. You guys gave me too much credit, 'cause my breasts aren't this big."

The majority of the laughter stopped and she scanned the mostly unfamiliar faces, pausing when she met Kip Claussen's eyes.

She pitched the undergarment into a wastebasket, embarrassed to be caught waving around a bra in front of the head coach. He'd warned her about this, and she'd been so cocky about being equipped to handle it. No doubt he'd report the episode to her parents, who would be more interested in how she dealt with the situation rather than who instigated it.

Kip swaggered past, clipboard in hand. "Well done, Charlotte."

Suppressing a grin, she issued a short nod of acknowledgment and finished checking in, meeting people she'd glimpsed at the team party but couldn't recall by name, as well as others for the very first time.

Of all the hands she'd shaken, the nods she'd returned, none had been Nate's. She didn't like compulsively searching a group for his face or that when she paused for a heartbeat, she remembered how it felt to have him against her, taking up her oxygen and replacing it with something that felt like uncorked lust. Nor did she appreciate the worry that lingered like a dark lullaby in the recesses of her mind, one that warned she couldn't trust a man with such an obvious motive to cause her family trouble.

Up to this minute he hadn't gone back on his word—her parents were all about action and would've contacted Charlotte by now if Nate had talked. So he was keeping *their* secret, or secrets if one also counted the heated-kiss-slash-wire-check encounter in the JW Marriott meeting room.

But for how long? Charlotte didn't know, and so she would be on guard, as Joey had cautioned. What she couldn't tell anyone, even her closest friends, was that one secret exposed would lead to another, then another, until her worst mistake resurfaced. Every minute now was an unknown.

All she could do was focus on the game.

Charlotte strode outside to be immediately signaled over to the sidelines as the players, damp from rain and sweat, dove into the first scrimmage, with Kip transformed into a hard, cursing force no one wanted to cross. Several minutes into the mock game, two rookies collided with a reverberating crash of bone and muscle and metal and hit the ground hard.

One man dragged himself to his feet. The front of his shirt was stained red, and when Charlotte and another trainer lunged forward, he hollered with his hands out, "It's his!"

Charlotte reached the injured man first, discovered blood blooming across his mouth and chin. As he reached back and yanked off his helmet, he growled a curse and she could see that he'd lost two teeth.

"Welcome to camp," the other trainer said with a friendly wink as they collected the teeth from the turf, and helped the player to his feet and off the field.

After the completion of the first of that day's two-a-day, Charlotte was refilling her water bottle at the Gatorade station when two offensive linemen trotted past in jersey shorts and cutoff tees, identical thick lines of sweat down their shirts.

"Rub on me anytime."

She looked up from the drink dispenser and brushed back the errant spirals of hair that had frizzed from the earlier light rain. "Who said that?"

"Said what?" the taller of the two replied, while the other shrugged and crossed his arms over a wide chest, making the Japanese characters tattooed on his dark skin soar over his biceps.

She glanced across the way at where Nate was crouched, examining one of the new prospect's quads. So far today, Nate hadn't said a word to her, and when he saw her now, as if he'd felt her eyes on him, he only turned his back to her and continued with his task.

So *that's* how it was.

Mind made up, she worked through the next few hours until the majority of the players had retreated inside to the locker room. Then, taking a deep breath, she barreled right in.

All of a sudden the same men who oozed confidence and felt free to say and do whatever they pleased on the field were modest and scandalized when she walked in on them without their pants.

It would've been laughable had Charlotte not been on a mission to defend herself and lay down some rules.

"Eh, somebody get her the hell out of here," someone shouted, and several booming male voices rang out in agreement.

"Nope." Charlotte planted her fists on her hips. "It's time for an anatomy refresher, don't y'all think? I am a female and you all are males. Our bodies aren't exactly the same, but so what? I'm not a massage therapist, so please do not try to be funny and ask me to *rub on you*. I'm a trainer. Let me do my job."

Several of the men had tuned her out and continued dressing—or *un*dressing—in front of their cubbies or moving off to the showers, while some cursed and others pretended to be invisible so that she wouldn't get the crazy idea to single them out.

"Nice speech. Now get out."

This came from TreShawn Dibbs. His shadow seemed to fall over her as he stepped closer, his mouth flat, his eyes cold.

Charlotte had faced down many a disgruntled athlete and wasn't going to back down from a man who'd been busted for steroids, found not guilty of cocaine possession and was rumored to have a history of domestic violence. In him her family saw championship potential. All they wanted were results.

Well, all Charlotte demanded was respect.

"Who said I was done?" she replied coolly, sliding her gaze about the room and seeing only bystanders who showed no interest in getting involved. Not even the men from the coaching staff, who for the most part wore poker faces. One—was he the wide-receivers coach?—was smirking.

"I did." Another step, then TreShawn reached back—

Charlotte's hand shot up, planted firmly on his chest with a solid *thwump*. Her heart surged against her ribs, but she didn't shake. "Touch me and you won't like what happens next."

Long moments later, TreShawn backed away from her and had the nerve to howl with laughter. "Made you flinch," he said, then tossed his towel at one of his teammates and left the locker room.

She waited, knowing he wouldn't leave the premises until after a full weight-training session. Checking his individual training schedule for the day, she made a mental note of when to be in the weight room. Time evaporated as she updated injury reports, viewed last season's films to compare the rehabilitated players' performances to what she'd witnessed today and sat in on the coaches' late-afternoon meeting in preparation for a full-squad training day tomorrow.

Charlotte had a few unscheduled minutes and took the opportunity to check her phone. A voice mail message from Tem marked Urgent.

"My sorority sister Rebecca's son, Chaz Lakan, is in the city tonight. He's a journalist in L.A. And he was an exhibitor at the Black Expo last year—remember? I told him you'd meet him for a late dinner...."

Her mother's message continued with the location where Chaz Lakan—the name still didn't sound familiar no matter how many times Tem had dropped it in her message—would be, and she was especially "helpful" in having taken the liberty of choosing the outfit Charlotte should wear.

Working the tension from her jaw, Charlotte put away her phone without returning Tem's call. Urgent, right. Pairing up her unmarried thirty-two-year-old daughter with a man was a downright emergency to her mother.

"You look pissed. Is it because of Dibbs or your phone, which has a talent for getting in the way of things?" Nate had soundlessly entered the room and leaned against his locker, watching her.

"The best way to forget the Rio is to stop mentioning it," Charlotte said. "Especially here. We can't bring what happened in Vegas to Mount Charleston."

"Right." He turned, opened the locker and swept off his shirt, rewarding her with a full view of his muscled, sweat-dampened back.

She was entitled to look, she told herself, so long as she didn't touch. And even that didn't seem fair, though she'd take what she could get. It was risky, but how could she not want to know, scene by scene, what would've happened with Nate had her mother's phone call not interrupted them in his suite?

Nate turned to face her, and suddenly she was unable to move. Holding her stare, he gripped a fresh T-shirt in front of him and took his sweet time putting it on, maximizing the effect that tickled and tortured her aching libido.

She'd never been more turned on to see a man change shirts.

"Charlotte," he whispered, his lips curving into a slow smile.

She blinked. "Uh…what?"

"Next time we do this, I hope we can switch places."

Any decent comeback failing her, she hurried straight to the weight room to see TreShawn exchanging bro hugs with the assistant coach who'd monitored his workout. When the coach left, Charlotte sidled up to the player. "So, TreShawn, how much better did you feel after intimidating me in the locker room?"

"Can't take it, then leave." Tough words, but there was no steam behind them as there had been earlier. First day at camp could wear down any man, and she thought it served athletes well to remember camp as a humbling experience.

He seemed especially drained, and she knew exactly why. There was a learning curve—physical, mental, emotional—when coming off steroids.

"Where are you going?" she asked.

"Damn, does it matter?"

"Yes." If he was desperate enough, he'd find a fresh hit of steroids. Withdrawal was one thing, but returning to a sport with a body that felt deflated compared to the way it had been under the effects of unnatural enhancements was something else entirely.

What kind of trainer would let him destroy his career and health that way?

Ask questions, get answers, push, watch over him. She would do it all.

"Miss, I'm going to get my hair braided." He reached up with flexing muscles and grabbed the big puff of tightly curled hair that was straining against a rubber band. He was known in the league for sporting long braids with a streak of color that was a shout-out to whatever team he was on. Now that he was the Slayers' new kicker, she assumed he'd be getting some red or silver in his hair.

He didn't call her Charlotte, as she'd asked everyone to do, but "miss" was a start and was actually…respectful.

TreShawn sighed. "Look, you don't believe me? C'mon, then."

Charlotte narrowed her eyes but followed him as he continued out of the weight room toward the lobby. "Come with you?"

At her hesitation he scowled. "Yeah. Thought you'd back off."

A dare.

"Do *not* leave without me!" Charlotte called, already

racing back toward the locker rooms. He'd challenged her and she was more than ready to show him she wasn't to be trifled with. She grabbed her duffel and ran back half expecting to find the polished lobby empty, with only a vacant reception desk and the supersized photo collage of past Slayers in action.

But TreShawn remained where she'd left him, and with a conceding headshake said, "Let's go. Don't touch my radio."

Chapter 7

Granite-black with a wide body and custom rims, Tre-Shawn's Chevy Suburban LTZ was designed for looks, strength and dominance. The vehicle was a complement to the image the man projected. So was the deep-bass, spirit-digging rap that vibrated throughout the SUV's interior. Like his ride, the almost painfully loud music spoke for him—angry, distant, a ruthless warning to be careful not to get too close.

Charlotte recognized his tough-guy facade for what it was and let him sink into the shallow comfort of it as he leaned back in the leather driver's seat, one platinum-ringed hand at the wheel. His posture relaxed, he seemed to have forgotten that she occupied the seat beside him, seemed to see only the stretch of highway before him, missing the series of pointed looks she shot his way as the speedometer's needle swept past eighty. If the vehicle hit a pothole, it would probably go airborne and God only knew how it might land.

Junipers and ponderosa pines blurred to nothing but a tangle of color. Up ahead, clouds seemed to drape over the mountaintops and felt close enough to grab hold of. She twisted in her seat, resolving to stare at his profile until he acknowledged her. The defiant set of his jaw and the furrow of his brow made him appear older, but he was close in age to her sister Martha. He was still a child in many ways, yet in others he was an old soul, one who'd grown up much too soon as a teenage delinquent.

"Gonna tap out?" TreShawn silenced the blaring rap with a press of a button on the steering wheel and flicked her a glance.

The quiet was so sudden it felt like whiplash. "No. But here's the way I see it. You're driving like a maniac with the intention to either scare me, in which case you've failed pathetically, or to piss me off, in which case you've succeeded with flying colors."

"You're in *my* space." At least his foot eased off the accelerator.

"Then next time be careful who you invite into your space. You keep thinking of things to throw my way, hoping I'll back down or give up." Charlotte shifted around to watch the Mount Charleston mountain landscape gradually transform into urban Las Vegas. "So. Are you always this combative to perfect strangers?"

"Why not? Eventually it's every man for himself. Even when somebody says they got your back. They never do."

The SUV, the rap, the aggression—it was all his armor. "You're in the NFL, TreShawn. Along the way somebody had your back."

"My uncle had a meal ticket. Cashed me in to Texas A&M."

"So your childhood was what? All rainy days, no rainbows?" It was the same way she'd reason with Martha, who could be stubborn and one-sided and wore a mask to hide her vulnerabilities. "No good days?"

"Pizza days were all right," he said thoughtfully. At her puzzled headshake he went on. "That Pizza Hut reading program. My school had the hookup—you know, read a quota of books, write reports and sooner or later you get a certificate for free pizza. My uncle made sure I kept at it, raised me to never turn down the chance of a free meal."

Charlotte figured his uncle's motivations had more to do with getting TreShawn educated. Clearly it had worked to some degree, because "pizza days" were the young man's rainbows. "Texas A&M put you on track."

"There's stuff you learn on the streets that you can't learn in the classroom, miss."

"The cocaine?"

"Wasn't my stash. Nor was the jacket the cops found it in."

"The domestic violence?"

"Ex swings at me, I block her, she falls and it's domestic violence."

"The steroids?"

TreShawn was silent for several heartbeats. Then, "All part of staying in the game. Sometimes you gotta do wrong to make things right."

"You won't be happy that way."

"Too grown and too real to chase happiness. You gonna tell me you made all the right choices?"

Charlotte snorted, her headshake solemn. "Hardly. But, TreShawn, please take it from me that the wrong things, they stick with you. You never forget them."

The young man shrugged as if to be nonchalant, but Charlotte saw the way his fingers tightened over the wheel.

"Miss, at the end of the day, football's all that's left. If I ain't got football, I ain't got nothin'."

That resonated. For so many people professional football was just entertainment, *just a game*. For others—people like Charlotte and apparently TreShawn Dibbs—it was life. Was it life for Nate Franco and his family? Or merely a slice of the image they wanted to portray to the world?

With a press of a button, TreShawn resumed the chest-pounding rap and ended the conversation. Charlotte let him be, satisfied that he was obeying the posted speed limits. When they rolled into an industrial-looking cranny of Vegas, she paid attention to the beautifully raw graffiti on buildings, the chalk on the sidewalks, the various ethnicities of people crisscrossing in the streets.

He parallel-parked the Suburban in front of a squat brick-fronted building, and Charlotte gazed up at the sign. Heaven and Hair.

"Georgiana hooks it up for me." TreShawn patted his big puff of hair again. "This will take a while."

"I have time." And unread work emails downloaded onto her iPad, for when the waiting made her crazy. And the "Fruit Ninja" app for when the emails made her crazy.

TreShawn set his vehicle alarm, then dap-greeted the vendor stationed in front of the salon frying something that smelled like Italian beef and fresh jalapeño peppers—something that promised to guilt her into an extra hour of early-morning running should she succumb to an everything-on-it sandwich. Charlotte let her willpower propel her into...

Whoa.

The sleek high-ceilinged lounge entertained the salon's waiting customers with high-definition news coverage and piped-in R & B set at a low, almost soothing volume. Turning in a slow circle, Charlotte took in the ultramodern details, from the stainless-steel beverage counter to the silver-glazed floor.

Abruptly she stopped. Someone was watching her closely. A dark man with a ropy build and a Mohawk braided from front to back hitched his chin in a wordless hello, then moved past her to the beverage counter.

"Who's that?" Charlotte asked TreShawn when he entered the place. "The man over there who looks like he's auditioning for an *A-Team* reboot?"

"Q."

"Just Q?"

"Yeah. He's security. Come here often enough and you won't even notice him. He's kinda part of the decor," he said, drawing out the last word, amusement evident in his eyes. "C'mon. G's waiting."

Beyond a pair of massive glass display cases containing hair-care products and tools was the pulse of the place. The spacious room was a harmony of color, complementing and contrasting in both muted and bold shades of gold and black and silver. Two rows of stations with ergonomic styling chairs sat in front of well-lit floor-to-ceiling mirrors. A large decked-out nail spa held pride of place in the center of the room. Modest-sized stations with plushy chairs encircled the revolving tower of nail polish bottles.

Over the cacophony of voices and music, TreShawn scanned the clients and heavily made-up stylists, then went over to a woman dressed in black except for the slash of electric-purple lipstick.

"What's goin' on, G?"

"Nothin' but the rent. Got your chair ready, and the weave you want braided in for that red streak." The woman who had to be Georgiana blinked at Charlotte. "Who's this?" she asked him.

"A trainer."

Georgiana frowned, skeptical. "For the Slayers?"

Charlotte introduced herself, unable to resist adding that she herself had partaken in competitive sports growing up and had trained college athletes. "TreShawn let me tag along today. I've never been here. It's an amazing place."

"I like to think my shop's the diamond in this rough neighborhood," the stylist said, seeming pleased with the thought. When TreShawn settled in at Georgiana's station, she gestured for Charlotte to take the adjacent styling chair. "Now Boo can do a little somethin'-somethin' with your hair. Hey, Boo!"

Charlotte opened her mouth to protest but right away another stylist appeared at her elbow, already eyeing Charlotte's untamed high ponytail, a utilitarian minimal-effort style her sister Martha dubbed the "half-assed updo."

TreShawn must've caught her hesitation, because as he adjusted his black cape, he said, "Never mind, y'all. She's not staying."

Another dare? The man just wouldn't stop testing her. What would it take to prove she wasn't going to haul ass out of the salon, that she wasn't going to abandon him when clearly abandonment was what he'd become accustomed to?

"You didn't come up in my shop and sit in that chair and think you were going to walk out of here with your hair lookin' like that, did you?" This from Georgiana.

The other stylist—Boo—vanished but reappeared not a full minute later with a thick binder. Her own hair was neat, with a deep side part and single short braid. "I do a few hair shows—just came back from Atlanta. Met Usher out there, too. Take a look at my handiwork, then decide whether you want to try a change. Nothing permanent, just something new."

All around her, people were choosing relaxers and highlights, hair extensions and thermal treatments, braids and finger waves. Charlotte appreciated the state of her hair, that it had natural shine and bounce and didn't require much maintenance. She ran six mornings a week and sweat came with the territory in her job, so stopping in once a month at Martha's preferred celebrity spa for a trim usually suited her fine.

But what was wrong with wanting something new?

Charlotte stopped perusing the album halfway through, in awe of the unique, futuristic hairstyles Boo had created. "Braid it, please," she said, then arched a brow at TreShawn. *There. I'll take your dare and raise you one.*

"Then let's shampoo you and get this party started," Boo declared, clasping her hands together with giddiness in her eyes. Immediately she unwound Charlotte's updo, revealing nearly two feet of loosely curled tendrils. "Ever straightened all this?"

"Relaxer in college. It turned out to be a mistake." Cloudy memories in the recesses of her mind intruded, and she swallowed to regroup. "Anyway, I did the Big Chop and left it alone after that. Jojoba oil's my lifesaver."

TreShawn sat with a sullen look for the next several hours, conversing in friendly tones only to Georgiana and Boo and a few men who'd come in for fresh linings. Clients came and left, and darkness had already settled in the sky before Boo finally turned Charlotte to face TreShawn and Georgiana.

"Boo, you're badass." TreShawn, who'd been showing Georgiana YouTube videos on his smartphone, now studied Charlotte with a grin—one free of malicious intent and snark.

Charlotte took her feet off the styling chair's rung, planted them on the floor and whirled around toward the mirror. *Badass* couldn't quite do justice to the transformation. Cornrows curved delicately across her scalp, with the ends of the braids falling together down her back in dozens and dozens of straight, skinny dark ropes. One braid, on the left side, close to her ear, was outfitted in a string of dark red beads. It gave the style a dash of playfulness but was no less exotic. Beautiful. Tough…

"Trippy," Charlotte whispered, running her fingers through the ends of the braids.

"It's like those Bo Derek cornrows she wore back in '79," Georgiana said with approval. "Or was it '80?"

Boo angled a handheld mirror behind Charlotte's head so she could view the back. "What do you think?"

Charlotte had come here to prove a point to TreShawn but wound up with a surprise of her own. "I found my new salon."

In Desert Luck's parking lot, Charlotte grabbed her duffel, hopped out of the Suburban and was halfway to her Fiat before she noticed TreShawn hadn't driven away. He'd put up a fuss with her every step of the way today, and she'd expected him to flee like a bat out of hell at the first opportunity. Turning, she moseyed back to the passenger-side door and motioned for him to lower the window. "What's keeping you?"

"Habit. My uncle said when you drop off a chick, wait till she's safely inside before you take off."

Charlotte didn't take offense to being referred to as a "chick." He hadn't meant to be derogatory. "Appreciate it, but I've been fending for myself a *lot* longer than you, TreShawn. I have a nice uppercut. I'm talkin' 'Mortal Kombat' style." At his grunt of laughter, she pointed to the building where a handful of straggler players and security guards were exiting. She waved and got mostly curious looks and one or two waves in response. "Plus,

I've got security. So enjoy being free from me. I'll be back in your face soon enough."

"All right." With that, the Suburban pulled out of the lot and Charlotte felt a degree of acceptance that today she'd done the best she could for the struggling young man. Tomorrow he'd be back at the facility to fight his demons all over again.

She didn't waste more time getting in her own car and hitting the road—except for the few minutes she took scanning the vehicles in the lot, curious—no, hopeful—that she'd see a certain man's James Bond–sexy Mercedes-Benz coupe among the remaining cars. When she didn't, she continued on to Vegas and resolved to put Nate and her questions about where he might be at this moment out of her mind.

Despite the late-night hour, her parents were wide-awake to greet her when she slipped inside the Bellagio villa.

"Joy to the world. The prodigal daughter has returned," Tem said, her voice saturated with sarcasm as she unfolded her slim figure from where she'd sat curled up on the oversize sofa in a couture summer dress. Little things like how she refused to lounge around in comfortable clothes even in her own living quarters just to keep up appearances were what made Charlotte sometimes think of her as a paper doll—beautiful but nonetheless two-dimensional.

Marshall, seated on the coffee table in front of his wife, turned to study Charlotte over his big rock of a shoulder. "Something wrong with your phone?"

"Pop, Ma, I've been working." Oh, how she regretted the defensiveness, the uncertainty in her tone.

"This late?" her father asked, rising to his feet and turning to face her full-on.

"Well. You could say I put in overtime."

Tem squinted, as if she suddenly no longer recognized her eldest daughter. "Your hair… What happened…? You…" She grasped Marshall's sleeve, wrinkling his shirt. "This is a joke, right, Marshall? You and I—we just got Punk'd."

Jeez. "It's not a joke. I was looking after a player and got my hair braided, spur of the moment, and it's not a big deal. Besides, I like it."

"Me, too." Martha poked her head around one of the large potted tropical plants near the full bar. She was disheveled from sleep but no less interested in what all the commotion was about. Exactly like how it'd been when they were children and Charlotte was reamed out for some misdeed or another. Danica and Martha would pretend to hide out so they wouldn't catch their parents' wrath, but the two would manage to linger close enough to eavesdrop on every word of their big sister's castigation and punishment.

"Go back to bed, Martha," their mother said dismissively, as if Martha was five and not twenty-two.

"Fine." With a huff, Martha took heed. As she stomped off, she added in a singsong loud enough to stir the dead, "Charlotte, you look h-h-hot."

"Ignore your sister," Tem told her, a queen giving precise orders. "A frivolous girl like that you take with a grain of salt. Come now, Lottie. Why did you stand up Chaz Lakan? Didn't you get my message?"

"Ma, I had work to do." And okay, *perhaps* a tiny part of the reason she'd leaped at the chance to watch over TreShawn Dibbs was that she'd wanted a solid excuse to turn down another unwanted setup with a man she had zero interest in—professionally and especially personally. "If you want me to succeed in the job you hired me to do, then please don't throw obstacles my way. Fighting off obnoxious man after obnoxious man is a distraction I don't want." She already had her hands full with a smokin', chiseled, wicked man who was the best—and worst—kind of distraction.

If she was going to get any sleep at all that wasn't disrupted by the memory of Nate teasing her with a view of his physique in the staff locker room, then she'd better get started on it now. "I'm going to bed."

Marshall halted her with a frown. "You're this dedicated, huh, Lottie? You're all in? Great. Then I expect to see this level of dedication from you always. Nothing less."

Charlotte bit the inside of her cheek to keep her angry response to herself. As if she needed yet another reminder that just because Marshall and Temperance Blue were her parents didn't mean they wouldn't take pride in being the bosses from hell. They would dangle what she wanted most—her career—in front of her and take glory in watching her jump to get it.

"Another thing." Tem sidestepped her husband and smoothed her hand down Charlotte's head, from her crown to the ends of her braids, lingering on the red-beaded one. "I told Chaz that you'll have dinner with him next week at DiGorgio Royal Casino. When you meet him there, be the woman he expects to see."

Because what people see, *their perception of me, is all that matters, right?*

"Your friend Krissy O'Claire sent a congratulatory bouquet. It's in the kitchen. She turned out to be a good egg. Isn't she engaged?" Not expecting an answer, Tem tapped Marshall's wrist and together, as one, they moved past their daughter toward their sleeping quarters. "Good night, Charlotte."

Charlotte had anything *but* a good night and had wasted an hour of it dwelling on things she should've said to her parents in the heat of the moment but knew she never would. In their own way they were just ensuring that she was capable of surviving in a world that could be crueler and more unforgiving than they could ever be.

Still, she left for camp in Mount Charleston just after daybreak. Utilizing the training facility's jogging path didn't do the wonders for her mind that her usual route at Cathedral Rock did, but she was ready to pour plenty of energy and concentration into the first full-squad day.

Midway through morning warm-ups, invitation-only media personnel invaded the practice fields, and as columnists and photographers milled across the sidelines tossing comments and questions to anyone who'd pay them any attention, the coaches and players completed the drills uninterrupted.

"Coach," Charlotte said when Kip called a break and the sweat-drenched men scattered across the field. She sprinted over to him and lifted her sunglasses to the top of her head, though he kept his firmly in place. These were a pair of Diesel glasses. The Maui Jim glasses he'd broken earlier when their new quarterback, Brock Corday, botched a snap. "Those defense boys have been cooling their heels for a while. I want to try something."

Kip turned his face in the direction of the men chatting on the sidelines. "What?"

"Yoga." When he rolled his shoulders and seemed ready to shoot down the suggestion, she rushed on because taking initiative meant sometimes crossing invisible boundaries. Implementing yoga into the daily workouts and diving deep into head-injury and helmet-safety research were her immediate plans and she didn't have time to waste. "Several teams in the league have incorporated yoga into their training routines. These guys are tough, yes, but they're men, not machines. It's not in their best interest for them to sit idle in the heat for long periods of time. They should use the elements. They should stretch and focus on strength as well as strategy."

After a moment he lifted a corner of his mouth. "Go get your boys. But run it past Whittaker first. Then maybe we can chat with the strength-and-conditioning guys."

"Whittaker…" she repeated, craning her neck to locate the head trainer, Whittaker Doyle, among the throng of people. And there he was, in a conversation with Nate.

All of a sudden she was ten degrees hotter, feeling as though she were trapped in a steam room rather than the fresh outdoors of Mount Charleston, which offered cool gusts of mountain air that Las Vegas didn't. She mumbled thanks to Kip and approached the men, reminding herself that she couldn't realistically avoid Nate and it would be no one's fault but her own if she let tension and nerves affect her professionalism.

As she joined them, she tripped over the turf but maintained balance. Even so, Nate sprang to catch her biceps and murmured, "Cool?"

Polite and collected despite the arousal that shot through her from fingertips to toes at the contact, she ducked away with a stilted, "Of course. I want a word with Whittaker."

When she shared her idea with the trainer and asked for his input, there was a skeptical pause before he replied, "What the hell, give it a shot. *One* shot, and we need to see results."

"If it works, would you support me in proposing yoga as a permanent part of the team's workout regimen?"

"I'll consider it."

That was a start. Excited, she adjusted her sunglasses, grinning at both men. Well, she couldn't alienate Nate without *someone* noticing. Only, he didn't return the amicability— just watched her as if she were a puzzle to be figured out.

"Will we see you on the court later?" Whittaker asked her.

"The court?"

"Nate's idea. Basketball tonight—staff only." The man frowned slightly in confusion, likely wondering why she seemed to be in the dark.

Their truce wasn't meant to be a one-way street. Nate wasn't going to get away with ignoring her by excluding her from something as innocuous as a staff basketball game. "I'll be there."

After convincing all but two of the available defensive players to try yoga, she was chased down by a cable-network sports reporter who complimented the *statement* Charlotte's hairstyle made and demanded commentary on TreShawn Dibbs's health all in the same saccharine sentence.

"A few sources said you'd be an authority on Dibbs's physical condition." The reporter tilted her mic toward Charlotte, awaiting a response.

"As a trainer I can share that we're all committed to ensuring our team is healthy and capable. If you want further comment, please have a conversation with a member of the coaching staff. Otherwise, stay tuned for an official statement from Dibbs's publicist or the Slayers' PR department."

The reporter gave her a shuttered look, clearly unhappy with Charlotte's version of a give-nothing-away answer. Changing tactics, she inquired, "What is the workplace dynamic with rivals among the Slayers training staff? Are you and Nate Franco playing nice?" She added a laugh, but her demeanor came off as facetious.

Charlotte was glad to see Whittaker waving her over but couldn't resist having the final word. "We don't play. We work."

Even engaging in a game of basketball with Nate was going to be less about *play* and more about working toward some level of compromise for the good of the team— and their careers. She had to remember the big picture....

Which was excruciatingly difficult to do later when all she could see as she made her way to Desert Luck's outdoor basketball court was Nate. Shirtless under the twilight sky, his gray athletic shorts revealing a pair of leanly muscular legs. It didn't take much to imagine him naked. On the court. With her underneath him.

Good grief. Charlotte dragged in a deep breath and tracked the off-key sound of a terrible Lou Rawls impersonation to one of the assistant coaches. About a dozen or so men had shown up, and upon her arrival the singing and cursing and sly talk and horsing around came to a stop.

Don't take it personally. Even though it's personal. Because you're a woman. The thoughts wouldn't leave her. Not when she was chosen last out of the lineup. Not when the designated ref ignored her shout of traveling against an opponent. Not when she went in for a layup only to be swatted down like a fly.

"Foul," Nate growled as she hit the pavement and grunted from the sting across her torso where she'd been struck.

Charlotte blinked, stunned to see him pushing past the wide-receivers coach, Royce Davis, to offer her a hand up. They were on opposite teams, but her men were more interested in mopping their faces with their shirts and guzzling Gatorade.

"That wasn't a foul," Royce protested to Nate. "I blocked her shot. What she did was flop." He glowered at her. "But if you want your free throws without any big bad men getting in your way, then let's call it a foul and get on with the game."

"Forget it," Charlotte said to Royce as she let Nate haul her upright. "No foul."

"Are you okay?" Nate asked, near enough that he could drop his voice for her ears only. "Tell me if you're hurt."

A sizzle danced over her flesh, and her mind spun. First he wanted to exclude her. Now he wanted to protect her. She couldn't quite figure out how to handle him when he continued to nudge her off balance at every turn.

"No harm. No foul." When a teammate passed Nate the ball, she drove the point home by proceeding to try to strip him of the ball.

Covering him was no easy feat. The man could move—pivot, fake, dribble. When he reared up to shoot, her arm tangled with his and his back met her front, two currents of heat colliding. The ball fell away in a succession of echoing bounces and others scrambled to rescue it from landing out of bounds.

Charlotte was so close to Nate that she knew the second his body tensed.

"That's it," Nate announced to the group in a strained voice, and was immediately answered with objections. "Play if you want, but I'm out." Already he was walking away.

Bewildered by his sudden change, Charlotte stood still on the court until someone tweaked her shirtsleeve on his way past her.

"Hear the man? The game's over."

Maybe the game on the court was over, but as for the one that was just between Charlotte and Nate that had no clear rules or definition?

Far from it.

Chapter 8

Be firm.

Easier decided than done when the person Charlotte needed to be firm with was her own mother. Almost out the villa door for an arranged date with Chaz Lakan at the DiGorgio Royal Casino, Charlotte froze in the foyer with the keys to her Fiat in hand. Even at this degree of frustration, she couldn't justify walking out and slamming the door with Tem calling after her.

"Lottie! The driver informed me that you canceled his services for tonight," Tem said, sweeping into the foyer. "Is Chaz picking you up here?"

Charlotte jangled the keys. "I'm driving myself. Thought it'd be lovely to have some semblance of control over this evening, which you thoroughly arranged without my input or permission. Ma," she went on when her mother's eyes narrowed in offense, "you have to realize it's not healthy for you to set me up with men. I can throw a rock and hit a man. Really."

Tem assessed her critically from her slicked-back bun to her one-shouldered fuchsia satin Lanvin dress to her strappy high heels. "Actually, I doubt it'd take even that much effort. You look sensational." She sighed as if to say, "More's the pity." "Finding men isn't your problem. *You're* your problem. You're choosy and stubborn—"

"And not divorced, like Danica. Or obsessed with collecting guys to prove how popular I am, like Martha." This time it was Charlotte's turn to sigh. "You act as if my being single is a nail in your coffin when the truth is you want to control what and who I do."

"Don't be crude. I'm not impressed."

"No news there. Nothing I've ever done has impressed you. Look, all I'm saying is right now I could choose a man to be with and you would hate my choice." Snap, snap, snap, where'd that come from? Logically she had no right to even think she could choose to be with Nate Franco, though she wanted him for a bazillion reasons that had absolutely nothing to do with bringing him home to meet the 'rents.

"Who would you choose, Lottie?"

"Forget it. I'm leaving now, in my car, because even though I'm doing this whole arranged-date thing with Chaz Lakan, I will come and go on my own terms."

Tem watched her silently for a long moment. "Give my best to Chaz. His mother's a friend and she'll want to know that my daughter is a civil person who doesn't make a habit of standing up perfectly eligible men. It's *de mauvais goût*."

"Ma." Charlotte reached out, grasping Tem's arm to reassure herself that her mother was still real and not truly as far away as she seemed. "I'm going to slip up now and then. But you have to trust me to make my own choices. And I love you. Pop, too. Okay?"

Tem smoothly twirled in her designer pastels, disengaging herself. "The builder's waiting for me to call him back. Fingers crossed, but the house just might be finished before midseason."

At least Charlotte had stayed firm. But driving herself to a casino for a date she didn't want was a small victory compared to her failure to get confirmation that yes, at the end of the day her parents still loved her.

The DiGorgio was a top-tier black-tie casino. From the chandeliers dangling overhead to the overabundance of leather and crystal in the Mahogany Lounge, the place screamed money. Charlotte considered partaking in a lively blackjack game but wasn't feeling particularly risky and bypassed the gambling rooms to order a Scotch neat at the tinted mirrored bar.

When the bartender added a potent shot of flirtation with her drink, Charlotte pretended not to notice and turned on her stool to face the room. Men in suits, women in dresses and jewelry—they all appeared to have come here for a high-stakes experience. There was something about the casino—maybe the lighting or the dark-colored walls or all the opulence swirling in the atmosphere—that encouraged you to be daring.

Charlotte decided she liked this place. With a silent toast, she nursed her Scotch.

"He *was* hitting on you. The bartender." A blonde in a lower-than-low-cut silver halter dress settled on the stool beside Charlotte and crossed her legs. "In case you didn't realize that."

"Oh, I did," Charlotte clarified conspiratorially, "but I don't have the best luck with bartenders."

"Too bad." The woman subtly glanced back at the man,

then faced forward as Charlotte had done. "He's attractive. They say once you're engaged, you're technically not allowed to notice other men, but this ring wasn't *quite* sparkly enough to take away my eyesight. Not to mention my fiancé's too preoccupied high-rolling in the VIP room to notice I left. So, what are you in for?"

"Waiting for a date. Journalists are said to value punctuality, but he's late…which actually doesn't surprise me." According to her mother, Charlotte had stood Chaz up. That he might return the favor wasn't too far-fetched. Yet she was curious to find out if he'd called, and she unzipped her handbag to root around in the dark for her phone.

"This might help," the woman said, retrieving a pink pig key chain from her own purse. With a press of a button, the thing oinked and flashed a beam of light.

When it aided Charlotte in locating her phone, which had slipped to the bottom of her bag, the woman insisted she keep it.

"I won't miss it. I have one in every purse. Now… where'd that good-looking bartender go? I'm in need of a whiskey sour." After she ordered and claimed her drink, the woman lifted her glass for a toast. "To women who wait around for men even in the twenty-first century."

"Cheers," Charlotte said, though she probably couldn't be heard over the ruckus at the end of the bar. A group in coordinating-colored formalwear was jeering and downing shots. "I'm Charlotte."

"Bindi." On the verge of saying more, she was interrupted with the arrival of Chaz Lakan, a suave-looking man who wore a pinstriped suit and oozed a practiced charisma. As he offered to buy Charlotte a drink, Bindi hastened to stop him with a grip on his arm. "No, that won't do! Ladies don't like to get all gussied up only to be kept waiting. Fortunately, I know a way you can make it up to her."

Frowning at the stranger who had the nerve to put a hand on him, Chaz replied, "You are…?"

"The woman who can get you into the Titanium Club."

Chaz's expression transformed from irritated to intrigued, which heightened Charlotte's skepticism about the offer. Furthermore, who exactly was Bindi to have the authority or desire to pull strings at a five-star casino for a pair she'd literally just met? "Isn't entry to the Titanium Club by invitation only?" Charlotte asked.

"Yes, and I've invited you. My fiancé and his family are hosting a celebration there. No one but absolute VIPs are welcome. Come up and get your luck on."

"Then we shouldn't intrude. It was nice of you to invite us, but—"

"Show us the way," Chaz cut in. To Charlotte he said, "Getting my luck on in the Titanium Club? There's no better place to be tonight."

Charlotte could think of several alternatives, none of which included an elite gambling room or Chaz Lakan, who now seemed more interested in admiring Bindi's short hemline than the woman he'd come to the casino to meet. To arrive late and straightaway jump at a stranger's invitation spoke his message loud and clear—he had as little interest in this setup date as she did.

But to keep her word to her mother, Charlotte joined him as he followed Bindi, who shimmered under the building's extravagant lighting in her silver dress and tall shoes. In the elevator he talked and bragged and boasted about his career, hobbies and accomplishments. Charlotte was so focused on tuning him out that she hardly noticed when the doors opened to an elegant top-floor corridor that ushered them into the Titanium Club.

Charlotte didn't plan to stick around long but didn't mind losing herself just for a while in the luxury of the high-limit gambling enclave: Art Deco style, enticing table games crowded with ritzy guests, polished servers moving soundlessly over the plush glittering carpet, the scent of liquor and cigar smoke and risk in the air.

"What's the celebration?" Charlotte asked Bindi as Chaz strutted off toward the poker table. They went to the bar, where Bindi requested a fresh whiskey sour along with a server attentive enough to make sure her glass didn't turn up empty tonight.

"A birthday in the family." The woman drank with relish.

A familiar figure moved into Charlotte's line of vision. He hung back, observing the two women even while the one who'd accompanied him tried to snare his attention. Again Charlotte felt a shudder of attraction at merely seeing Nate. How he seemed able to coax an intimate reaction without actually touching her at all was beyond comprehension.

Bindi followed her gaze. "You're staring at that guy."

"Um." She squared her shoulders, determined to keep Nate where he belonged—in the category of coworker. "I work with him."

"I see." Bindi wiggled her fingers at Nate, and Charlotte wanted to shrink, hoping he wouldn't come up to them and play yet another round of "Guess Who I Am Today." One minute he was with her, the next, against her—and not in a good, hot way.

Nate's response was to take his date's arm and stride off to the roulette wheel, which was whirring as fast as Charlotte's thoughts. Even when she wasn't looking to find him, the man continued to make appearances in her life.

Discreetly she searched for him in the crowd and spot-

ted him now fully occupied with three different women—
one of whom was an Emmy Award–winning actress.

"Meet my fiancé," Bindi suggested, crooking her finger at someone.

Charlotte almost choked to see Alessandro Franco coming toward them. *He* was the woman's fiancé? Charlotte
must've overlooked that nugget of information when she'd
surfed the web for information about Nate, but uneasiness
colored her shock. Why hadn't Bindi mentioned that she
also knew him?

In person Alessandro Franco appeared almost gaunt,
but he commanded attention, dominating the room as he
greeted Bindi with a nibble on her neck.

"You doing good over there, Al?" Bindi said, turning
fully into his embrace.

"Molto bene."

"Winning's put you in a fantastic mood. Imagine if you
got lucky every night."

Unsure what to say to that, Charlotte kept her mouth
shut until Al released his fiancée and inquired, "Who's
this *bella donna?*"

"Charlotte Blue," Charlotte answered, watching for
his reaction. He slid Bindi a sidelong glance—was that
disbelief? Disapproval?—but when neither he nor Bindi
commented, she continued, "Now that you know who I
am—who my parents are—will you have security escort
me out?"

"That would be cruel, considering what measures you
must've taken to get into the club to speak to me."

"Actually, I was downstairs waiting for a date and Bindi
invited us up. Now that the opportunity to speak to you
has come up, yes, I'd like to, Mr. Franco."

"Call me Al. It's my firstborn's birthday. Drink in his
honor, won't you?" Without pausing to let Charlotte de-

cide, the man ordered port for the three of them—though Bindi made a show of nudging aside the port and favoring her whiskey.

"Port for you, *bella* Charlotte."

"I don't know if I've acquired the taste for it." But she accepted the glass anyway. Could she possibly reach Nate via his father? On the surface Al seemed reasonable, if reserved and a tad on edge. Nate needed to know that his father had willingly initiated the sale of the Slayers franchise to her parents. Okay, so perhaps this wasn't the opportune time or place, but— "Can we talk?"

"Please do."

"I meant privately." Maybe it was a moot point to ask for privacy, particularly since his fiancée had been the one to extend the invitation to her in the first place, but there was a hungry, predatory air about Bindi as she secured her hold on Al and watched Charlotte with a neutral expression. Even if Charlotte did ask, it wasn't likely that Bindi would leave Al's side. Whatever else she had to say to Al Franco, she'd have to say it in front of his fiancée.

"Is there any chance of the Blues and Francos getting along?" Gently she added, "Your sons have the idea that my parents—my *father*—coerced you into selling the team."

When he simply stared at her, unblinking, much as her mother had earlier, Charlotte felt frustration surge through her system. "Whatever my father said to you has been misunderstood. Marshall Blue's a big guy, and yes, he can be intense. Everyone knows that. Some people find it charming. But he'd never put himself on the line by threatening a beat-down just to buy your football team."

"What do you want from me?"

"I'm looking to move forward," she replied. "Maybe to start I ought to find my date and leave."

"Stay. I insist."

"Al, my family doesn't want any trouble…. My parents are both good people—"

"Charlotte Blue," Al interrupted, untangling himself from Bindi and preparing to walk off with his port. Not *bella* Charlotte. Just Charlotte Blue. "A word of wisdom. You're only as good as the worst thing you've ever done."

"Why is she here, Bindi?" Nate had earlier downplayed his surprise at spotting Charlotte in the DiGorgio Royal Casino's private gambling den—decorating the bar with Bindi Paxton, of all folks—but as he pretended interest in the roulette game, he watched his father join them for a drink and soon after saw Charlotte abandoned by Al and Bindi.

Bindi, who appeared to be in a celebratory mood despite the little detail that it was the birthday of a man she despised, had worked the room in her silver look-at-me dress and had eventually made her way to the roulette table. Picking up one of his chips, she muttered, "Know thy enemy."

Nate turned to spy Charlotte in the recesses of the room, sitting at the poker table with her date, a man in a pin-striped suit. Bindi dropped his chip, upping his bet, which was promptly lost to yet another house victory. "Don't try your luck with my chips, Bindi."

"Sorry." But her eye roll contradicted any contrition. "I recognized Charlotte in the lounge and had to get her up here with Al. Just like I thought, she started right in on pressuring him to tell you and Santino that the sale is legit. All she cares about is her agenda."

Couldn't the same be said for Bindi…and him? Nate shook off the thought. He was only hunting for a solution to a problem, righting a wrong. Thankfully, Santino, the guest of honor, was in the club dining room with his date—not that even an elaborate meal prepared by a celebrity chef could fully distract him from the truth that he was another year older but no closer to recovering from the loss of his career in the NFL and his birthright.

Nate had asked his college friend Elaine, who'd graciously agreed to be Santino's companion on his birthday, to be extra patient. Sometimes having friends as close as family came in handy. Elaine, and their friends Vaughn and Jayda, had been happy to join the Francos tonight. Science geeks in college, the four were so tight that they'd kept in touch after graduation despite the fact that Nate had declined a lucrative offer to study in a prestigious PhD program in order to pursue a career with his family's pro football team. It had been his opportunity to impress, to prove he was no ordinary nerd. Vaughn and Jayda had paired off and gotten hitched, but Nate didn't have any designs on Elaine.

Nate was dateless tonight, having been more concerned with ensuring his brother had a good time. Besides, he got more than enough female attention on a regular basis and was comfortable with that reality. Or he *had* been before he'd crossed paths with Charlotte.

She was his worst temptation. Being around her every day at camp was glorious torture. She made him feel like a naive boy, and he was anything but. He wanted to prove that he was stronger than basic lust, needed to resist the impulse to protect her.

She was bad for him. Just as Bindi said, Charlotte had her own agenda and wasn't afraid to put it first. At camp he'd observed with his own eyes her assertiveness…how she acted as if she believed "It's me against the world" yet could be vulnerable if caught off guard. During that staff basketball game, when the wide-receivers coach had knocked her to the ground, Nate had seen that flash of vulnerability cross her face. And when she'd let him help her up, he'd felt glad that she trusted him truly for just those brief few moments.

Man, did he have it bad. What he needed was to clear his head, maybe let one of the perfumed beauties in the Titanium Club distract him from his ultimate distraction.

After all, Charlotte had clearly moved on to someone else.

"Who's the man she's with?" Nate asked Bindi.

"Chaz Lakan, a journalist from la-la land."

"You brought a *journalist* here without clearing it with the owner?"

"Hey," she said defensively, "the only reason Charlotte is even up here is because the guy was all for it. Just tell DiGorgio to keep his high rollers on their best behavior if he's worried about bad press. What's the problem, anyway? This is a casino. People gamble and drink and smoke and hook up. Big deal."

Nate didn't want to make waves in the casino. He'd wager the Girard-Perregaux wristwatch he wore tonight that his godfather, Gian DiGorgio, wouldn't like the idea of media infiltrating his private, excessively guarded gambling den. Everyone here tonight, from A-listers to politicians, had an understanding. Gamble dirty, socialize freely, and nothing leaves the club. Oh, and, of course, no unauthorized media allowed.

That Bindi had broken a rule, had disrespected the casino owner's wishes just for the chance to toy with Charlotte, showed Bindi's desperation—and made Nate just a tad unsettled.

"The outcome is all that matters," Bindi said, reaching for another chip from his stack. "If we can take away Charlotte's power, remove her as a threat and show her parents that we aren't kidding around, then we're pretty much guaranteed to get back what belongs to us."

Pretending to lean down to examine his chips, Nate said carefully, "Bindi, the team's not yours. Never was."

"I don't know what you and Santino think I'm after, and frankly I don't care. Your father made a promise to me. He can't honor it without reclaiming the team."

"What if he gets what he wants but still reneges on that promise? What then?"

Bindi handed him back the chip, her eyes flat. "I'm in this, Nate. Are you? Because if you are, you can't question me at every turn."

Nate glanced to where Charlotte and her date sat at the poker table. His imagination conjured visions of her claiming the head trainer position—he'd already witnessed her in conferences with their superiors on the training staff and coaching staff regarding her push to bring yoga into the Slayers' training regimen.

Then his memory interfered, adding images of her hard at work with the players and arming herself with confidence in the face of disrespect. Simultaneously she was a threat to be defeated and a prize to be won.

Either way it wasn't right, because she was more than even that.

"Nate? What's it going to be?"

Tuned in to Charlotte, Nate sensed her laughter. He saw her toss her head back, chuckling at something the pinstriped journalist said. "I'm in," he told Bindi, easing away from the game. "Bet it all if you want."

Nate made his way to the Titanium Club's packed dining room and claimed a seat at Santino's table. On one side of him was their father. On the other was Santino's date for the night, Elaine. "Good party, Dad."

"I wish I could take credit," Al said, clapping Santino's

shoulder, "but it was Gian's suggestion. So all compliments go to him. And according to him, all complaints and the bill come to me."

Laughter followed. Then, when Elaine excused herself to the restroom, Al reached over to straighten Santino's bow tie with a smirk. "My son. See that?"

Santino and Nate exchanged confused shrugs.

"Elaine. She looked back at you when she left for the powder room."

"So?" Santino reached for his wineglass but Al stopped him.

"Listen. Every woman I've had a…deep connection with…from Gloria to Bindi, has looked back at me in a crowded room. Elaine looked at you."

Nate didn't appreciate his mother and Bindi being lumped together that way, but his father was insistent upon making the point that his college friend Elaine was genuinely interested in Santino and just maybe… "Is this a prediction of some sort? That Santino and Elaine might end up getting serious?"

"A possibility. The odds are in your favor, Santino. What do you think of that?"

"I think it's time you switched to something zero proof." Santino took their father's wineglass and replaced it with a crystal goblet filled with ice water. "I know Charlotte Blue had a chat with you and Bindi. She's still here. Why?"

"Our conversation was brief. Bindi says she invited her to the club to gamble, so let her gamble."

"Maybe someone should keep an eye on her."

Nate waited until the chef delivered the main course from the menu he'd personally prepared for Santino's table before he slipped out of the dining area to the spacious gambling room. He saw Charlotte engaged in a lively blackjack game, her date nowhere in sight. He strode over.

"Of all the gambling joints in all the towns in all the world, she walks into mine." He met her flustered look with a poker-faced expression and hovered behind her as a fresh round of bets were placed and the silk-vested dealer began whipping out cards.

"Bogie. You own this casino? And here I thought seeing you tonight was just a kooky coincidence." The dealer dished out a ten to accompany Charlotte's nine and four. Giving up on the game, she moved a couple steps back from the table, allowing a man in a tuxedo to take her place.

Nate did not move, and now she was wedged against him. The blackjack game was getting hot and folks were converging from all corners of the room. He used that to his advantage, wondering how long he could have Charlotte right where he wanted her. "I don't own it. My godfather does. Earlier today at camp you mentioned looking forward to having time to yourself. Yet here you are. Would we really call you and I being here tonight a coincidence, Charlotte?"

At the sound of her name being whispered across her ear Charlotte seemed to shiver. She looked different, so tame and exquisite. At camp she always showed up dressed to work hard and sweat plenty—and more than once this week he'd been struck with the urge to pull her into a private corner on the training estate and kiss her until all his pent-up want transferred from his soul to hers. She deserved to know what he faced every single day.

"First of all, alone time is a wish that's hardly granted. I drive practically forty miles every morning for a daybreak run at Cathedral Rock, mainly to get away from duties and expectations and…everything. And second of all, your stepmother invited my date and me up here."

Emphasis on the word *date*.

"Bindi's not my stepmother."

"That's a formality. Something tells me you're not her biggest fan."

"We have an understanding," he said carefully as the sway of the gathering blackjack crowd bumped him closer to her. "She didn't accept my father's ring because she's interested in playing the mommy role for two men who're older than she is. How many stepmothers wear dresses that seem to be held in place by magic?"

"Not magic," Charlotte murmured, his nearness making her shift like a nervous cat. "Very strategically placed adhesive. Well, she does have redeeming qualities, like perfect teeth and generosity."

"Generosity?"

"She gave me a pig flashlight. I have to say I wasn't sure about her…. She didn't tell me right off that she knew you. I thought she might not be on the up-and-up. Anyway, it makes sense now, seeing as how you and she apparently don't get along." A roar erupted from the table, and Charlotte leaned forward to see the excitement, bringing her firm ass right against the front of his trousers. Without thinking, without even breathing, Nate slid his hand over the fluttery fabric of her fuchsia dress to splay his fingers against her belly. Inconspicuously, shielded by tuxedos and party dresses, he fit her to him.

Charlotte turned her face to the side. If she made a move to get away, he would let her go. But if she wanted to stay, to remain locked to him…

"One minute you don't want me around. The next you want me."

Even whispered, the words were risky to say aloud in a crowded room. That she'd taken such a chance compelled him to react in kind, match her risk for risk.

Nate's hand ventured lower, from her abdomen to a

place that teased his memory, bringing him back to the Rio, to those moments in which she was his.

Charlotte inhaled deeply as he smoothly slid his hand upward. "The basketball game. You quit out of nowhere."

"Because of this." Nate rolled his hips against her behind, and she gasped faintly even as her body automatically arched back to meet him. The intensity of the blackjack game escalated, the room heady with a collective rush of adrenaline and endorphins. Repeating the hip roll motion slowly once more so he could savor the tautness of her abdomen under his hand and the suppleness of her behind hugging his crotch, he said, "Maybe the reason I don't want you around is that I want you too much."

As if unnerved by his words, Charlotte said tensely, "I have to go. Part of the gamble is knowing when to walk away." Scooting around him, ready to flee, she dropped her hand and Nate caught it, automatically weaving his fingers through hers.

A series of groans and protests shot up as the dealer claimed another win. And when Charlotte squeezed Nate's hand before pulling away and rushing off from the crush, he suspected he'd screwed up and lost a part of himself to her.

That detail wasn't confirmed until he spied her hurrying out of the Titanium Club with her date following close. At the door she turned sharply as if she'd forgotten something, then settled her gaze on Nate.

She'd looked back at him.

A blinding succession of flashes and clicks was a disorienting reminder of why he couldn't just go charging after Charlotte and figure out a way for them to explore what they mutually desired—without everything else falling apart.

Two men with cameras prowled the place like wolves

invading a sheep pasture. Paparazzi. Uproar ensued, and Nate, along with his father and godfather, assisted security in muscling the pests out.

On a suspicion, he sought out Bindi in one of the shadowed recesses of the room. "Paparazzi, Bindi?"

"Uh, you're welcome." Unfazed, she sipped from her wineglass. "I'm just keeping you and your family relevant. Trust me, when things get ugly in Team Franco versus Team Blue, you're going to want to have the media on your side."

It would be virtually effortless to let Charlotte take the heat for Bindi's machinations, for him to let the battle begin and prove to his father that he was capable of saving their family, but Nate couldn't let anyone doubt that in this situation Charlotte was innocent and hadn't brought the paparazzi with her into the Titanium Club. Yet coming to her defense this time wouldn't change the truth that she was still a Blue, still a trainer bent on conquering his territory....

Still a woman he wanted but couldn't have.

Chapter 9

It was dark, clouds forming a soft gray haze in the sky, when Charlotte rolled off the comfort of her mattress to see a silhouette darting across the villa bedroom. "Martha?" she said around a yawn, twisting the knob on the nightstand lamp.

Dim white-gold light washed the room. No longer concealed by shadows, Martha froze—in the same jeans and floral-patterned bustier top she'd been wearing when she'd gone out the previous evening. "Well, you have bed hair but probably didn't get it sleeping."

Martha shook out her hair, going over to her designated pajama drawer in the dresser they shared. "Why does it feel like you're accusing me of something?"

"Not accusing. Observing." Charlotte cracked her neck and turned to smooth her bed linens, not so much to make sure she had a well-made bed to come home to but to give Martha privacy to change. Her sister wasn't modest and had a particularly aggravating habit of throwing propriety to the wind whenever the mood hit. "Bed hair aside, it's almost four in the morning and you're just getting home."

"Didn't think you'd notice, since you were so busy getting dolled up for your date with that Chaz dude. He was all Ma could talk about. Chaz this, Chaz that. Gag me."

Charlotte heard her sister flop on the bed with a sigh and knew it was safe to turn around again. "Ma pushed me into that date. It's my own fault for letting her. But, Martha, I pay attention to you even when you think I don't." She got out of bed and gathered Martha's strewn clothes off the floor and deposited the pile in the adjoining bathroom's hamper. "Who's the guy keeping you up all night?"

"Lottie, the better question is, why isn't there a guy keeping *you* up all night?"

Refusing to be baited, Charlotte made quick work of her early-morning ablutions, threw a loose purple crew-neck shirt over her sports bra and fitted shorts, then grabbed her running shoes and duffel from the closet.

Martha's whisper sliced the silence. "About Ma and Pop. If they ask where I've been—"

"I'll tell them I don't know." Charlotte shrugged and turned off the lamp as she prepared to go. "It's the truth, after all."

"Right. If Claussen gives you a decent break today, why don't you come by the stadium for lunch? You haven't even seen my office yet. It has a window. With a view. I feel very important."

"I might take you up on that."

"Good. Then we can hash out why you turned down *Maxim* and still haven't made a decision about *Sports Illustrated.* You should be all over this. It's a chance to tell the world what you want to accomplish in sports training. *And* you'd get to show off your runner's bod."

"In what? A string bikini?"

"What's wrong with that?"

Charlotte sighed. It wasn't about shyness or camera fright. It was about the importance of what she had to say and how easily provocative photos could overshadow that, especially if word got out about her recent hot history with Nate Franco. She was new on the professional-sports scene, and her mother had warned her during the Slayers' team party that everyone was watching.

Everyone was indeed watching, yet no one could agree on who they wanted her to be. Magazines wanted her to be sexy. Her players wanted her to be a trainer who'd take their crap with a smile. Martha wanted her to be cooperative. Danica wanted her to be careful. Her parents wanted her to be their statement. Nate Franco wanted her to be...

She couldn't be sure, especially after last night at his godfather's casino. And that pissed her off. She needed to be clear where she stood with him. He said he didn't want her around because he *wanted* her. How was she supposed to react to that?

"Say yes to *Sports Illustrated,*" Martha encouraged. "If you're asked to wear a string bikini, so what? Rock it. Use it to your advantage. Give them a killer interview, and make Ma and Pop proud of you. Sometimes I think that's your endgame in all this—getting their approval for once."

She wasn't in sports to please Marshall and Tem. In fact, she'd defied their wishes and the "more appropriate" paths they'd pointed out to her. "I'd be lying if I said I didn't want to prove them wrong. They don't think I can train our boys."

"Or stand on your own without some guy they've cherry-picked for you." Martha nuzzled her face into her pillow. No doubt her makeup smudged the pillowcase but she was evidently too tired and carefree to let it bother her.

"We're whispering in the dark, like children. As long as I live under their thumb, I'll never grow up." She yawned. "Go run. Good night. Or good morning. Whatever."

The Fiat was damp with drizzle by the time Charlotte pulled onto NV-592 W. Fidgeting with the radio channel search button, she bypassed KNPR, which usually kept her company during her morning drive to Mount Charleston, and left it on a station playing talk-free hard-core hip-hop. Many people clung to this flavor of music; some found inspiration in the poetry of the words. But after a full set that closed with a posthumous Tupac hit, she jabbed the power button and let in the quiet.

The music hadn't helped her compartmentalize the thoughts and anxiety that surged through her mind like floodwaters. The pressure to protect her career and her parents' team battled against her urgent need to make all the personal choices she wanted, screw the consequences.

As she drew closer to Mount Charleston the rainy darkness gave way to a foggy dawn. The stretch of road up ahead was still fairly visible and wouldn't get in the way of her south-loop eight-miler. As a precaution, though, when she parked outside the closed-gated Cathedral Rock picnic area, she grabbed a slim flashlight from the glove compartment and jammed it into her waist pack along with her phone, drink bottle, lip balm, pepper spray and keys.

At this time of morning there were rarely any visitors, even in the areas that remained open twenty-four hours. There was nothing but the scent of rain-dampened foliage colliding with that of a doused forest fire's lingering smoke, the scenic views of aspens peppered along the steep trail, the sounds of tiny creatures scurrying about in the underbrush and her shoes hitting the ground hard, the pounding of her heartbeat and the cool air against her damp skin as she ran at a steady pace.

Concentrating on the incline of the trail and the adrenaline flowing through her system, she pretended to outrun her worries about work and family and the man she couldn't avoid—and didn't want to. Made believe that for this pinch of time she was alone and free. Imagined that there weren't a grain of truth to Alessandro Franco's "word of wisdom" last night.

You're only as good as the worst thing you've ever done.

Charlotte had never claimed to be "good" and didn't find it fair that her career and her parents' perception of her depended upon how perfect she could be…that the worst thing she'd ever done, no matter how irrelevant to her professional abilities, could cancel out what she'd done right.

"Deal with it, Blue." And she ran faster.

About a mile later, at a sharp bend in the trail, she stopped for a stretch and a healthy sip of her diluted Gatorade. Fog moved around her and through the trees like translucent ribbons. Securing the drink bottle in her waist pack, she took off around the bend only to drop into a crouch at the sound of rocks and twigs crunching under someone's heavy footsteps.

Pepper spray was good. Her uppercut—even better. Satisfied with that, she compensated for the limited visibility by focusing with her ears.

More footsteps.

She waited. Better not to break the jaw of a hiker or even just another runner.

"Charlotte."

Automatically she sprang up and let loose a series of expletives.

Nate's form parted the billowing fog. Arms raised, palms out, he took another step forward. In jeans and a wrinkled gray tee, he looked scruffy. "How much longer you plan on yelling?"

"Um. You nearly scared the bejesus out of me, so, yeah, I'm entitled to a little yelling." Charlotte paused to inhale deeply because she'd apparently been holding her breath while evaluating the threat. "By the way, you came *real* close to getting a face full of pepper spray or my fist, and if either of those had happened, you'd be the one yelling. For mercy."

Nate lowered his hands, considering her words. "There's something hot about a woman who can fight for herself."

She schooled her features into an impassive expression, not willing to let him throw her off guard. "It's what I do best." Around them the woods were quiet. It was unusual to encounter another visitor on this route at sunrise. "So. You hit the trails now? And here I had you pegged for a gym addict."

"Weights at my place, but when I need cardio, I take it to the streets. I always figured the city was as good a place to run as any…" Nate cast a glance upward at the scenic view "…but maybe I can get why this is your hideout."

"A Vegas girl like me can appreciate some peace and quiet every now and then. This trail's easy enough to handle before a full day's work, and the best thing about it is that it's practically a ghost town before the place fully opens to visitors. Every once in a while my sister Danica joins me, but usually it's just me and the birds and occasionally the Palmer's chipmunks."

"The what?"

"Palmer's chipmunks. Ascend high enough around here and you're likely to spot one. They're striped, typically stick close to the ground and consider this little region their hangout." She leaned forward and smoothed a wrinkle on his sleeve. "Nate, did I even tell you I run Cathedral Rock?"

"Last night at the casino, you mentioned driving way out here to get away from expectations. So this is what you do—come here at a crazy-ass time of morning to run, then hit the showers at Desert Luck? And before you ask, I know you shower at the facility every morning because your hair's always wet and you smell like that flowery stuff you shampoo with at the end of training days. That fragrance follows you everywhere.... I heard a coach say the staff lounge has never smelled so good."

"Rose hips and jojoba."

"Powerful stuff. It could boost morale."

"Doubt it. That's more about player-to-player relationships, solid man management and whatnot."

"Then maybe it boosts only my morale."

His heated stare fastened on hers the way his hands might pin her wrists to a mattress.

"Nice detective work," she managed to get out. At least her voice was strong and not all swoony or shaky.

Nate edged closer. "Still, it wasn't easy to find you in the middle of all this. I lost time searching the north loop. I was about to give up when I saw your car outside the gates."

"Well, you interrupted my run for a reason. What is it?"

"Paparazzi crashed the Titanium Club minutes after you left. Camera flashes lit up the damn place like fireworks...but the memory cards are now property of Gian DiGorgio. It doesn't erase the fact that a few wannabe TMZ minions ended up in my godfather's private club on my brother's birthday."

Charlotte straightened, ready to jump into defense mode. "Like you said, that happened *after* I left. I'm not tight with the paparazzi. Blame anyone you want—just not me, because I had nothing to do with it."

"I know you didn't, Charlotte."

It took a long moment before she absorbed the magnitude of his words. "Despite my showing up with a journalist and then having a not-exactly-friendly chat with your father, you believe me?"

"Yeah. But you can see how someone could interpret those facts as proof that you have an ax to grind and set this up. That someone being my father."

"Fantastic. So by simply accepting his fiancée's invitation to the club, I've given your father ammo to make even more outlandish accusations against my family?"

"No. I told him you weren't involved in it. That I kept track of you."

Charlotte stilled. The memory of standing at the blackjack table with Nate's fingers pressed against her, his body hard behind her, stunned her with a burst of euphoria that was laced with frustration. Once again they'd begun something they couldn't—shouldn't, *better not!*—finish. "Did you tell him *how* you kept track of me?"

"Saw no reason to get into specifics. Just know that he's aware the paparazzi stunt isn't your fault. I'll admit he didn't want to accept that at first, but I persuaded him."

"You did that for me?"

A muscle ticked at his jaw. Clearly he was very carefully selecting his response, as if navigating a minefield. "It was the right thing to do."

Charlotte jerked her chin in a semblance of a nod. She could thank him and walk away or stay and find out if the desire she'd felt in his touch and voice last night was still alive in the light of a foggy day. *Leave it alone,* her saner self warned even as the words tumbled from her lips. "Do you always do the right thing?"

His gaze dragged over her, as erotic as a lick on bare flesh. "Not always."

"You didn't have to get up at the crack of dawn to find me here. We could've discussed this at camp."

"Camp doesn't really offer me the opportunity to take you...aside for private talks." His deliberate pause wasn't lost on her, and the slow tilt of his mouth at her nervous swallow made it evident that he damn well knew it. "So I had to take initiative."

"Whose bed did you leave to come out here at such a 'crazy-ass' hour, anyway?" There, she'd asked in a sort-of-frank, sort-of-veiled fashion whether or not he was sleeping with someone, at the same time wondering why she couldn't keep from poking at that hornet's nest of lust between them. But there was plenty of time for regret later.

Now was the time for curiosity.

"My bed. In an apartment that's mine and mine alone. You're not the only one with a hideout." Nate ventured closer. She held his gaze, slowly moving off the trail and deeper into the canopy of trees, and he was keeping up with her...joining her in the foggy semidarkness.

"And that journalist of yours. Where is he?"

"Why do you want to know?"

"When you were leaving, you looked back at me. If you were so into that guy, you wouldn't have turned around at the exit. But you did."

"The journalist isn't mine, and I haven't seen him since we said something to the effect of 'Have a nice life' in the DiGorgio parking lot and I drove myself home. I went out with him to please someone who can't be pleased." Charlotte gripped the front of her waist pack tightly to keep her fingers from reaching out to slide along his angular jaw and over the hard muscles that lay beneath his shirt. "What do you want from me? Everyone wants something, and if what you want is something I can't give, then you should know now."

"I want to see you. Not trainer Charlotte. Not the Charlotte who dresses up for a man she doesn't want to be with. I want to see *you*."

"Newsflash. This is me."

"Okay." Keeping his gaze on hers—oh, God, it sizzled through her defenses—he reached behind her with one hand and deftly unlatched her waist pack. It met the ground in a soft thud, and there was nothing in the air but a dense mist and an unspoken dare she knew she wouldn't pass up. "Then just answer this. Why did you look back at me last night, Charlotte?"

The emotional face-off came raging forth. What to reveal? What to hold back? But in honesty she found escape. "Because I wanted to stay. With you."

Charlotte wasn't lying to him. Nate's intuition told him she was for real. Tuned completely in to her, he sensed her boldness and hesitant trust. She wasn't after a fantasy with some stranger. She was making a choice.

Despite what was at stake for both of them, they couldn't seem to keep away from one another. Before, he'd told himself he had the excuse that he hadn't known the identity of the woman he'd taken up to his suite at the Rio. But now he couldn't pretend not to know. He'd gone after her. He knew exactly who she was, what she wanted and how finishing what had jumped off at the Rio would be both his best and worst decision ever.

The plain, cold facts warred with hot lust in his mind, and he had to make a choice. Now.

Nate hooked a finger into the elastic band reining in Charlotte's hair and drew it down until her curls tumbled free. He replaced the elastic with his hand, tunneling it through until he could cradle the back of her head. "Stay, Charlotte."

"Don't…"

Immediately he started to release her, to back off.

She laughed lightly, using the back of her hand to mop away the shimmer of sweat on her forehead. "Don't call me Charlotte. Call me Lottie, like you did before."

React. That was all Nate would do. There was no need to calculate or plot. There was only instinct and touch and demand. He went for her bottom lip, tasting the soft swell before penetrating her mouth with his tongue. Her groan vibrated in his mouth, and in turn he explored his fill— gently sinking his teeth into her lips, learning the texture of her mouth.

He let her go and she gasped sharply, crossing her arms protectively across her chest. He'd shocked her. Good. "Lottie."

The naked joy that lit her face nearly brought him to his knees. Her arms fell, then swept up in a single grace-ful movement, the hem of her purple crew-neck shirt tangled in her fingers. In seconds the shirt was floating to the ground and she was in front of him in a black sports bra, shorts and an inviting smile.

She burrowed her anxious hands beneath his shirt, re-discovering the shape of him, her fingertips bumping along his abdominal muscles, then skimming up his back until her palms were pressed to his shoulder blades. "At the hotel…it was, I don't know, unreal. But I never forgot your body and how you touched me. Did you forget?"

No way. He'd tried to, because forgetting would've made it easier to put things in perspective and manage working with her through hellishly long training days with-out fantasizing about losing his mind and kissing her on the practice field.

To answer her he stepped out of her embrace, peeled away her bra and slid his splayed fingers up her damp skin to cup her breasts. She closed her eyes only to open them again—wide—at the sensation of his mouth closing over one of her nipples.

The taste of her elicited a moan from him, heightened his senses and sensitivity to her touch when she scraped his scalp with her fingernails. He retaliated with a firm grip on her behind, bunching the mesh athletic shorts and tugging them downward even as she toed off her shoes.

Charlotte dipped to shed her socks, then rose slowly, emerging from the swirling fog with that quirky, irresistible little smirk and dirty intent in her eyes. She was soft skin over toned muscles and killer curves. She went for his jeans, rubbing him through the denim, leaving it up to him to get rid of his shirt.

In the time it took for him to yank off the shirt, she'd unzipped his jeans and worked her hand beneath the waistband of his boxers.

Now she was the one shocking him, with her erotic, gritty promises and the way she raked her fingers up and down the length of his erection before baring his ass.

He sank, landing on his shirt and taking her down with him. Hovering over her with his pants halfway down his thighs, he fumbled for the condom in his wallet. As he searched her eyes for signs of retreat and found none, he pressed the condom into her hand. This wasn't about a power struggle or manipulation or competition. It was about Nate and Charlotte, giving and taking, finding the rightness in a situation that seemed to be wrong in a dozen ways.

As she was occupied with tearing open the packaging, he took the opportunity to curl his middle finger against the heat between her legs. She sighed, bowing up, opening herself further to his exploration.

He leaned, groaning into her hair at the snugness of her flesh around his finger. Relentlessly he teased her until she clenched and dropped back in a series of spasms, and then he let her test the weight of his erection in her hand before she rolled the condom onto him.

Nate captured the sight of her beneath him, her eyes hooded, her body moving in sync with his, and the feel of her welcoming him into her pulsing wet heat provoked a low curse that made her laugh in surprise.

"I knew it," she whispered on a deep sigh.

"What?"

"That this would be *good*."

Bracing his weight on his knees and one forearm, he grabbed one of her hands and pinned it to the ground beside her head. Then, with their moans blending and damp flesh meeting in rhythmic slaps, they let go.

Nate waited until she crawled away to gather her clothes before he righted his pants. There was an awkwardness to her movements. In a matter of minutes she'd gone from hotter than hell to colder than ice.

Shirt in hand, he walked slowly to her as she pulled up her shorts. He bent, pressed a kiss to the center of her smooth back.

"Nate. We're screwed."

He gathered a handful of her hair to expose her nape, kissed her there and got a deep, pleasured groan in response. "I know."

It was hilarious and shattering at the same time that in spite of all the trouble that could come out of willfully crossing the line together they'd done it anyway. And wouldn't mind doing it again.

Charlotte finally moved away to finish dressing, all the

way down to snapping the pack around her waist and chugging down a few swallows of her drink. "We've stirred up something between us, and it's not going away anytime soon." Distractedly, she offered him the bottle, unaware how sweet the gesture was. If either of them should slip and show affection like this in public, the coaching staff, the front office, the media wouldn't ignore it.

"If you weren't a Blue and I wasn't a Franco, this—" he pointed at her, then himself "—wouldn't be a problem. Gotta admit, this isn't the first time I've regretted who I am. I love my people, even though they can drive me batshit crazy. It has more to do with me and the choices I've made." He gave her a considering look. "Bet you've always been comfortable in your own skin, huh?"

Charlotte shook her head. "No, Nate. I'm pretty imperfect, and mostly I'm okay with that. I've made some poor choices, and there was even one time when I cut my hair off just to get over a *really* poor choice I'd made. It was all in the name of getting my way and sticking it to my parents, which sums up my college experience." She stiffened, as if stunned that she'd said as much as she had. "Anyway, it feels like too many people are waiting for me to mess up again."

He wanted to band his arms around her, touch her where she was most responsive until that worried frown melted into an expression of ecstasy. But he didn't. Instead he let her find her own composure and strength. "Charlotte, when we report to camp today, will anything be different in the eyes of the team?"

"No, because no one knows.... Hold up. Are you saying we have a shot at keeping this between us?"

"Yeah." He put on his shirt, glad that he had a spare in his duffel that wasn't dirtied with telltale signs that he'd been tussling around in the woods.

Chapter 10

Four training days passed before Charlotte wound up
alone with Nate again. Yes, she'd kept count. And yes,
she was hyperaware of him when she barged into the staff
lounge to toss her smashed Phiaton headphones into her
duffel bag. The pair was a casualty of a squabble between
a few defensive linemen in the cafeteria.

Nate had been on a call but cut off the conversation.

She held up the damaged phones. "Just tossing these
away."

"Jesus. What happened to them?"

"Two hundred sixty pounds of linebacker." Locker
open, she was busily stuffing the headphones into her bag
when she heard him ease the lounge door closed and en-
gage the lock. By the time she turned around, he'd already
crossed the room and was in front of her, hitching his chin
at the row of bottles on her locker's top shelf.

"Um. Are you a hoarder?"

"No," she denied with a laugh. It felt good to tease and banter, relaxed, especially after four days of torturous silence. Work had kept them busy, but it was after hours when she'd think about him and feel his absence most strongly. It wasn't that she was missing him, she told herself.... That would only introduce a whole new layer of complication neither of them was looking for. This closeness was supposed to be on the low, and temporary, until they could burn themselves out and move on.

But they had a habit of setting rules only to turn around and break them—along with rules set by everyone else.

For one thing, he'd locked the lounge door, which just wasn't done at this facility. Desert Luck's open-door policy was literal. Part of the new mission statement emphasized teamwork, and no team member had the permission to lock anyone out of any room, be it the auditorium, the conference wing, the training room or a lounge. Charlotte's only real privacy was the ladies' restroom, which she used only minimally in an effort to stay integrated with her colleagues.

And for another thing, she was letting Nate get too close. He was starting to reach her on a level beyond physical.

"So, what's up with all the shampoo bottles?"

Oh, *man,* the timbre of his voice did something wicked to her. Charlotte rose up on her toes, answering softly, "I heard it's gotten to be popular around here, so I stocked up on enough to get me through camp. Thought I'd do you guys a favor."

Nate reached out to shut her locker, then backed her against it and settled his hands on either side of her head. "That deserves a proper thank-you."

She dragged him forward, covering his mouth with hers. Coaxing a muffled groan from him, she snaked a hand into his shorts and underwear to grab his ass. "You're welcome."

"Lottie…there *is* something I want from you."

Instantly tense, Charlotte furrowed her brow. "What?"

"Your number." Nate's gaze dropped to her mouth, which was a bit swollen from their rough kisses. "Don't you think I've earned it?"

Obviously they weren't close to getting their fill of one another, and they couldn't continue taking risks like this at Desert Luck Center. They were on the brink of falling in deeper, strengthening an already powerfully dangerous connection, but she could save them both right here, right now if she just said no.

"Give me your phone."

When he grinned and handed it over, Charlotte knew she was in trouble.

"She's playing them."

Nate had to fight to control his instinct to defend a woman he wasn't allowed to step up for. Instead, he helped his brother settle into one of the leather chairs in the home theater as *SportsCenter* featured coverage from the Slayers' NFL Play 60 campaign event. Having spent most of yesterday guest-speaking at a UNLV seminar about musculoskeletal medicine, Nate had missed the chance to work with the children who'd been bused to the training facility to spend the day with professional athletes.

After today's semiformal dinner for the training staff, hosted at Whittaker Doyle's house, Nate hadn't bothered changing out of his suit before driving straight to Lake Las Vegas for a visit. Even though his father was out and his brother still in a foul mood from a grueling physical-therapy session he'd endured earlier in the afternoon, Nate had stuck around, hoping he and Santino could chill like brothers. Like how they had back in the day, when Santino had saved Nate's life and given him a future…before their mother died and their father fell into his ongoing downward spiral.

Would Santino make the same trip? Was it already happening? His spirits had been high on his birthday until the paparazzi had shown up. He hadn't responded to Elaine's messages, either, which Nate knew because she'd eventually told him so—adding the specific instruction for him to never set her up on another date, favor or not.

Nate focused on the team footage in front of him. Players in jerseys and coaches in red polos were interspersed among the other supervising adults as kids sporting Play 60 shirts littered the practice fields. There was a noticeable lack of women, which had plenty to do with the fact that the Slayers were one of the few teams that didn't have an official cheerleading squad. Despite the buzz about Charlotte Blue being approached to pose for magazines, and the owners' statement that they were "examining the pros and cons of providing that aspect of fan entertainment," it didn't look likely that athletic women in red and silver would be performing at Slayers Stadium this coming season.

The footage remained on Charlotte in a thin-strapped silver top and shorts, with a whistle hanging from a lanyard, demonstrating to a group of teens the proper lunge technique. When an overweight boy lost his balance and looked ready to stomp off in embarrassment, she trotted to him and repeated the steps until the group lunged cohesively. Then she gave him a high five and a wink, and let Doyle lead in her stead as she jogged out of frame.

It didn't seem to Nate that she was playing anyone. She was patient with those kids. And without isolating the boy who'd struggled, she'd given him the personalized care he needed to accomplish something as seemingly small-scale as a lunge. And that boy's smile as he slapped his palm to hers was all confidence, gratitude and adoration.

To an insecure teenager, a little attention from a beautiful female went a long way. Attention from a female who was beautiful *and* genuine was priceless. Nate knew the difference. Growing up he'd been strung along plenty by girls who'd used their looks and his hormones to reduce him to a human ATM and a schoolwork flunky. It was that genuineness he'd been starved of, and he'd eventually outgrown searching for it.

Until Charlotte, who fulfilled his wish list and was tough and sexy and wild on top of it all, found him. Just his luck she'd be one of the untouchable Blue daughters.

"I've been on the field with Charlotte," he told his brother. "That right there is how she really is. She leaves camp every night with the same energy she comes in with at six in the morning. Some of the guys have been assholes to her from day one, but she won't back down. She brings it."

"She's playing you, too." Santino swore, reached to rub between his eyebrows. Veins in his arm looked as though they might poke through his skin. He was hitting physical therapy hard, but though his form appeared fitter and more cut than during his last season in the NFL, his spinal damage continued to cause pain as well as limit his speed. "Charlotte Blue had no business showing up in the Titanium Club that night."

Nate twisted around to look at his brother's profile. When had Santino become belligerent, a man who'd rather hate and attack than build a new future for himself? Oh, right. When his career and his chance to inherit the Slayers franchise had been ripped from his iron grip. "Bindi said she invited her up."

"You're smart, damn it, Nate. She was there and *so were the paparazzi*."

"Drinks, fellas?" In a strapless summer dress and high heels, Bindi sauntered in, carrying a tray of what appeared to be an assortment of liquor bottles and glasses. Her eyes were sharp with warning as she bent forward to offer the tray to Nate.

Santino punched a button on the remote, making the massive screen go dark behind Bindi. "I can't take looking at one manipulative woman on the screen and having another dance around in my face."

"You don't know Charlotte like that," Nate said to his brother. "Ease up on her. Bindi, too." Santino and Bindi baited each other as if it was a game, but he didn't appreciate being dragged into it. Nor did he believe in sitting idly while his brother provoked Bindi. True, the woman was in a class by herself, but she was still a woman—his father's fiancée—and deserved a modicum of respect.

Nate declined the offerings, realizing they were all hard liquor. He had a long drive back to his "hideout" in Las Vegas, and judging from the direction his visit with Santino was going, he'd be tempted to down a random bottle all on his own.

"Pick your poison," she murmured, dramatically bowing before Santino with an indiscernible smile. "That's an expression, you know." When he chose Jack Daniel's, she set the tray on the glass-topped sideboard and approached them, chin raised, hips swaying. "Santino, I'm helping your brother get the Slayers back. When I saw Charlotte at the casino, I had to think on my feet. I wasn't going to say anything, but you insist on irking me."

"Bro, is she lying?"

"Tell him we agreed to this a while ago, Nate," Bindi

encouraged, though with a slight headshake. *But don't you dare tell him I got the paparazzi into the Titanium Club.*

"She's not lying."

Santino's gaze rose grudgingly up to Bindi's big blue eyes in acknowledgment—or perhaps apology—before snapping back to Nate. "What's the plan, then?"

Damn, there was hope in his eyes. It took the possibility of doing something drastic, with no concern for whom it affected, to restore his brother's hope. How screwed up was that?

Nate stood, as did his brother. "I don't know if there's a plan anymore."

At this Bindi cut in. "Since when? You told me you were all in. You want job security. You want the team to be given back to Al. Right?"

"Yes. But Charlotte can't give us what we're after."

"How do you know that?" Santino pressed. "Is she talking to you?"

Nate felt crowded and furious. "Back the hell off. Both of you. Charlotte's a trainer and from what I know, her parents didn't just hand her that position. Trust me, y'all aren't the only ones gunning at her." He pointed at them. "Each of us has probably made twice as many mistakes as she has."

"About her mistakes…" Bindi lifted a brow. "I have this feeling, Nate, that you're more acquainted with the skeletons in that woman's closet than you're letting on."

"We're grown-ass adults, and here we are plotting to screw her over just to get to her parents."

Bindi sighed. "Are you done with your tirade?"

"I'm done with this conversation." Nate shrugged to emphasize it. But it was his brother who angrily left the room, moving at a speed that was guaranteed to aggravate his spinal injury.

Bindi poured herself a clear drink. "You reneged, Nate. You said you were in this with me. An apology's not necessary. I just want you to realize that for all my faults and all the reasons you dislike me, *you're* the one who went back on his word. Guess that habit of breaking promises is something you Francos have in common." Her eyes were bright with determination and desperation. "I've depended on men, sure. But don't think for a minute that I can't get things done in order to survive."

Despite her provocative clothes and makeup, Bindi looked more like a scared, angry child as she turned and marched out of the room. The last thing Nate wanted was for her issues to become his concern, but it wasn't right for a woman young enough to be his little sister to rely on the money and success of a man twice her age—a man who spent more time in casinos than with her. In a way Nate had never comprehended before, he saw that Bindi and Charlotte were somewhat alike: spirited women who each thought life was about counting on no one but herself. But Charlotte wasn't so far gone that she'd taken to using people in order to get by.

Thank God for that.

To protect Charlotte he'd gone back on his word to Bindi, though. He'd broken an agreement that perhaps he'd had no business making in the first place. Bindi was no innocent, but he didn't feel good about becoming one of the many men who'd let her down.

Nate had cost himself an ally to spare Charlotte, a woman he could be with only behind closed doors…or in vacant woods. It was almost too crazy to be real. A science nerd's life wasn't meant to be complicated with deceit, secret sex and intrigue.

No, he didn't always do the right thing.

But this time, it felt as though he had.

Chapter 11

An early-morning radio interview with a local sports-talk station threw off Charlotte's schedule and set the tone for the day.

First she'd had to skip her run and show up in Mount Charleston a half hour late, including the ten minutes she'd needed to change clothes and twist her hair into a ponytail that the ladies from Heaven and Hair would have cringed at.

Next she'd had to work through lunch—breaking the routine she'd fallen into of eating with TreShawn Dibbs and a few other players who considered her to be "all right"—to cram in a midday yoga session with Mazzie Lindwood.

Mazzie was a chiropractor who'd driven in from Beverly Hills to aid in Charlotte's research and proposal, which she'd sworn to submit to Whittaker and Kip by the close of training camp. If all went well, the proposal would be passed up the chain of command and ultimately

yoga would be incorporated into the Las Vegas Slayers'
training regimen.

On top of her normal days at Desert Luck Center, she'd
been burning the candle at both ends to research and exper-
iment. So far her parents had "surprised" her at camp on
two occasions. Finding nothing to complain about, they'd
left her alone. She didn't need pats on the head or gold
stars. This was, after all, business. They wanted results,
and she could either deliver those results or she could find
another gig.

Then, with next to no time to spare, Charlotte was heading off the practice field when she was hit with another
injury case to treat and document. The second scrimmage
hadn't started and already at least eight men had required
medical attention.

Charlotte asked one of the other trainers to do her a
solid and meet up with Mazzie as she knelt to examine
the blood blister that had sent a rookie offensive player
to the sidelines. Blisters were painful, but right away she
sensed that the young man was using these minutes to regroup mentally.

"It's my first camp, too," she said as she applied a pad-
ded dressing to his foot. "I imagined it'd be tough as hell
to live through. But I was wrong."

The man frowned.

"It's worse."

"Fifty-three players by September," he said, lifting the
collar of his shirt to wipe his sweaty face. "Around the
damn corner. I know I can't make that cut."

"Nah, you don't believe that," Charlotte said. "A mas-
ochist would take on training camp *knowing* he won't
make the cut. Don't sit on my bench and lie about knowing you can't make it." Treatment complete, she held his
foot still and checked her work. "Here's my assessment.

You're fine to finish up the day. Then you need to elevate this. You're also tired and scared. So's everyone else. It's part of the game."

"Lottie."

She straightened to see Danica crossing the turf in a slim pantsuit with three-quarter-length sleeves. Sunglasses hid practically half of her face. "Hey, Danica. You picked a busy day to visit. Can we walk and talk? I have an injury report and a yoga meet—"

Danica cocked her head at the player, then said to Charlotte, "Come with me."

The sight of the general manager barreling onto the field had garnered more than a few curious glances. Charlotte didn't ask questions, but with each step the vibe that something was very wrong grew stronger. Especially when she scanned the field but couldn't locate Kip Claussen or Whittaker Doyle, who both were ordinarily *always* present. Somehow in the blur of faces she recognized Nate, who removed his sunglasses and squinted across the field, mouthing something she desperately wanted to believe was "I'll be here."

Inside, Charlotte sped up and blocked her sister. She'd known Danica since before she was born, and now the younger Blue daughter was leading Charlotte through the hallways as if she were a naughty child who had to be escorted to her punishment. "What's going down, Danica?"

"It's not a social visit. Please, just follow me and we can talk."

Four long halls later Danica opened the double doors to the film-viewing room. And it was crowded. Claussen. Doyle. Her parents.

Danica gestured for her to enter. Then she followed and shut the door. "It's come to the PR department's—and all of our—attention that you spent some off-field time with a team member, Charlotte."

Charlotte froze. They all knew. But Nate wasn't here. He was still on the field, and he'd seemed as confused as everyone else when Danica all but snatched her up. If he'd reported what they'd done, then he would have repercussions to face, too. Unless… Had he lied somehow?

Her heart screamed that it didn't make sense, but how else could her direct report, the head coach, PR and the front office know that she'd had sex with Nate Franco?

"I…uh…"

Danica put her glasses atop her head, walked to where their parents sat and touched their shoulders. "Charlotte, this will go much quicker if you just cooperate and give us the truth about your interactions with TreShawn Dibbs."

TreShawn Dibbs? "Wait, what's this about?"

Tem shot up then. "It's about sexual misconduct. Does that spell it out for you? People—our own guys—saw him drop you off here at this facility on the first day of camp. And the braids. You were photographed on the field wearing that hairstyle. You've been giving him extra attention since then."

"Ma. Oh, are you Temperance Blue now and not my mother?" Charlotte regretted the childish remark, and that she was losing composure in front of her superiors, but the idea that she was carrying on with TreShawn Dibbs was absurd. "I was concerned that camp might depress him, push him toward steroids again—"

Tem scoffed. "His contract prohibits steroid use."

"People hit crossroads. They get confused. They take risks!" *Careful, now.* Nate was her crossroads, her feelings toward him confused her, and she'd lost count of how many risks she'd taken to touch him in private and talk to him when no one else was around to hear.

"Continue, Charlotte." This from her father, who was reaching into his jacket pocket. Antacids.

"I rode with him to a hair salon in Vegas, we got the braids and he dropped me off in the lot. I am not sleeping with a player. Pop? Ma? How much more info about my sex life do I need to provide to my direct report and my coach?"

Uncomfortable, Kip Claussen looked to Marshall for instruction.

"This stays here," Marshall said to the coach and the head trainer, hitching his head toward the door. Once they'd left, he shook his head at Charlotte. "Want to know *my* concern? That this will weaken our men. This isn't just a team. Not on my dime. It's an army. If you're not a soldier I can depend on, then get off my front line."

"This 'army' should be more resilient to baseless gossip." She watched him rise from his chair, and he was such a big man to face off against that she almost shut up. "I'm not interested in Dibbs that way. He reminds me of Martha."

Danica scrunched up her face. "Martha?"

"Yes." She glared now and wasn't sorry for it. "If any of you knew TreShawn—knew *Martha,* for that matter—you'd understand."

The accusation hit its targets. As Tem and Marshall's voices rose in a flurry of offended remarks, Danica intervened. "Y'all made me GM for a reason, so please let me handle Charlotte. You can trust me."

"Always," their mother confirmed, then clasped Marshall's hand and left.

Charlotte's stomach twisted. "It's only a rumor, Danica. There'll be hundreds more. This is a nonissue."

"It's not that simple. I'm sorry, but it was careless to jump in that man's car and then show up to work with a hairstyle similar to his. A sleazy reporter suggested that your matching red streaks meant you were a couple."

A hysterical laugh bubbled forth before Charlotte could stop it.

"Administration's in hell with men holding out, stadium renovations and folks like Dex Harper not taking no for an answer, and you're *laughing?* Fraternizing with a player's funny? Are sexual misconduct and termination of employment funny?"

Charlotte stared into her sister's hard-as-steel eyes. "No. Nor is the fact that we wouldn't be having this conversation if I were a man. This double standard you and our parents have isn't making any of our jobs easier."

Danica crossed her arms. "The owners, Coach Claussen, Mr. Doyle and myself have discussed this and agree that for the time being, until the dust clears, you'll need to let another trainer deal with TreShawn Dibbs. On and off the field." She hesitated, then, "I'm begging you to keep your distance. He's trouble. You have a career to protect."

"But you hired him!"

"For results. For victories."

Finally Charlotte sat. More like collapsed into the chair. "No, Danica. I was getting through to him. He's not who he lets the world think he is. He needs encouragement and consistency. This man's grown up expecting everyone he trusts to turn their back on him. Don't force me to be just another person who's failed him."

"It's an action you have to take. Don't fight this. Do the right thing."

Meaning obey their parents' wishes. "Don't you get sick of being Ma and Pop's version of perfect, Danica?"

"You won't speak to your general manager that way."

Ah. So when backed into a corner Danica wore her title

as a shield. "So sorry. For a minute I thought I was having a conversation with my sister."

"At the stadium and this facility I am your boss."

"Why, Danica? Because it makes things easier for you? As GM you can robotically go along with whatever they say because it's only business, right? But as my sister you can't so easily justify following their every order. I'm not asking for preferential treatment. I'm asking for fairness."

Charlotte didn't realize she was trembling until Danica gripped her hands. "Claussen and Doyle are in your corner and I want you on this team, too. But Ma and Pop's choices trump everything. No matter how good you are, if they feel you're a liability, you're out. Please…just do as we've asked."

In other words, accept the decision that had already been made for her.

Nate was watching the field when a man's shout of agony brought everyone's attention to Brock Corday, who suddenly hunched and dropped to his knees. Getting to the quarterback in a short sprint, he pinpointed the site of injury—rotator cuff, or "My friggin' shoulder!" as Brock had exclaimed, his face contorted in pain. With the aid of a coach and another trainer, he guided the man to the sidelines as someone paged Kip. The head coach and head trainer hadn't returned to the field since before Danica Blue stomped across the field and retrieved her sister as if she owned the place.

In a way she did.

Charlotte hadn't returned yet. This wasn't good. Dread worked through his gut. At worst, administration had somehow found out about his intimacy with her, and at the end of the day he'd be out of a job. At best, Danica's business with Charlotte had nothing at all to do with him and he could continue seeing her—in secret. That option was better than the first, but not by much.

Charlotte was bold and took him by surprise and could set his body ablaze with just the right look. A woman like that shouldn't have to be tucked away or have to settle for a hush-hush relationship. He knew the secret paradise they were finding in each other couldn't last forever.

Nate tried to push his scattered thoughts about Charlotte out of his mind as he concentrated on tending to Brock's injury. When the man ceased his brutal curses and sporadic groans of agony, Nate placed a call to the physician's offices to alert them: quarterback down. The situation was easy to grasp. Significant damage meant Brock might face surgery and recuperation during the remaining exhibition games and wouldn't get in nearly enough practice to establish reliability for game one. The Slayers could be in deep shit, as the owners were banking on Brock, who had the skill and image they wanted to represent the franchise.

"Coach, where the hell have you been?" the quarterback growled as Kip raced to them, followed by Whittaker Doyle and Marshall and Temperance Blue.

"Taking care of a personnel situation. What happened to you?"

Brock explained how he'd launched the football and in the next instant had felt pain rip through his shoulder. Then Nate added, "It's his rotator cuff."

"A sprain? A tear? What?" Tem inquired, not satisfied with the limited diagnosis. "Whittaker, examine him. I want Brock on the field with a football in his hands for the next at-home exhibition game. Ticket holders aren't paying top dollar to get acquainted with our backup. He'll need to make an appearance."

"Tem, no one can confirm the extent of the damage without proper imaging," Whittaker told her, and Marshall grunted in agreement. "I taught Nate Franco. He's an award-winning trainer. His judgment's sound. You know that he's my second."

Nate pretended not to see her frosty look, though he was sure that only by some miracle had Charlotte become such a nurturing person. Tem had the warmth of an icicle in the back. "I called ahead to the docs. Let's get him inside and you can get the specifics."

As the quarterback was transported off-site to the hospital, the practice field began to clear as men trooped inside for showers and food. Nate found Charlotte in the weight room, relieved to see that they were at least momentarily alone.

"Any word on Brock?"

"Not yet. Whittaker said he'd get in touch with the staff when there's word, before anything's released to the media."

Charlotte nodded slowly. "There's a rumor that I'm involved with TreShawn Dibbs. It's probably more to get everyone hyped up and talking about the new season but at my expense. Anyway, the owners want me to steer clear of TreShawn for a while, until a juicier rumor about another team works its way through the media. I don't want to abandon him, but my choice is to either keep away temporarily or go against a direct order and get cut from the staff for noncompliance."

Referring to Marshall and Temperance as "the owners" rather than as her parents—there was something very wrong with that. "They cracked down a little hard, didn't they?" Nate remarked.

"It's their managing style," she said, her face void of the heat and humor that usually touched her features when they were together. "At first it seemed they'd found out about you and me. As pissed as I was about their overreaction to gossip, I was twice as glad that we could stay the same."

But they couldn't stay the same. He wanted to erase the line he and Charlotte had drawn in the sand regarding their relationship. At night he wanted to hold her. At work he wanted to be near her every chance he got. At parties and social events he wanted to have her with him, on his arm. He wanted to have her back, without costing her what *she* wanted: her career.

"We haven't burned ourselves out yet," she commented softly.

"Training camp's coming to a close soon. Are we going to take this into the season?"

Charlotte sighed. "Know when the best time is to worry about tomorrow?"

"When?"

"Tomorrow."

Nate clasped her hand as he had at the DiGorgio Royal Casino. "Then be with me tonight."

Charlotte left Desert Luck at eight-thirty, after the head coach pulled her aside and urged her to go home. "This was a tough day for you, Charlotte. The sooner you put an end to it, the better."

Problem was, the next day wasn't guaranteed to be any brighter than this one had been. That was why without objection Charlotte showered, threw on the beige lace flare dress and thin black leather jacket she'd worn for her interview and took off. She was determined to end today on a better note.

The text Nate had sent her asked that she meet him at eleven, so when she drove the Fiat into Las Vegas, she went straight to the modest ranch-style house that boasted a trio of palm trees on either side of the structure.

Charlotte rapped on the deep-green door with one hand as she used the other to root around in her duffel for the house key Joey had given her. Pushing the door open, she shuffled in, then set her stuff down in the living room. Even with no one home the place felt cozy and lived in, with vibrant wall colors, mismatched throws draped across the rich leather sofas, artwork that had been acquired not because it was popular or conveyed any specific message but because Joey simply liked it. Plus, it always smelled like fresh-baked cake, which was a mystery since her friend did not bake.

Charlotte was about to commit herself to crashing on the sofa for a good hour before meeting Nate.

Until a half-naked Greek god came swaggering out of the kitchen with a bowl of Froot Loops. Finding Charlotte frozen in place, the shirtless man cursed while fumbling to zip his pants, which barely hung on his hips. At the commotion Joey came limping in with her cane and stumbled to a stop in white panties and an unbuttoned LVMPD shirt.

Well, that explained where Parker the Cop's uniform top had wound up.

"Ay dios mio!" Joey shrieked, yanking the shirt closed. "Lottie, you cannot walk in unannounced on two people who are in law enforcement."

Charlotte smirked. "From the looks of it neither of you is carrying a weapon."

"Don't underestimate my cane."

"I did knock. You just didn't hear. I used my emergency-safe-place-away-from-crazy-family spare key to get in." She waved at Parker, who'd zipped up but appeared to be in search of something. "If you're looking for your shirt, Joey's wearing it."

"Thanks." The laugh he shared with Joey was candid

and intimate. They hustled down the hall and within a few short minutes Parker was dressed and heading out.

"I'm sorry, Jo," Charlotte said when her friend re-emerged in her own clothes and eating Parker's cereal. "I had no idea he was here. I didn't see his car."

"He parks it in my garage."

"Get out!" Eyes wide, Charlotte rushed to the picture window to see a squad car backing out of the driveway. "You're obsessively picky about who you let park in your garage."

Joey munched on a spoonful of Froot Loops. "I'm sensing a double meaning to your use of *park* and *garage*."

Charlotte grinned, moving away from the window and into the kitchen for a bottle of Evian. A pen-and-ink still-life drawing secured to the refrigerator with a D.A.R.E. magnet took her attention. Popping back into the living room, she perched on the arm of the sofa where Joey sat. "Amazing picture on your fridge in there. Who's the artist?"

"Parker's son. He's learning crosshatching in an art program."

"Josephine de la Peña. Congratulations. You're hooked on this cop." When Joey opened her mouth to deny it, Charlotte listed the facts. "You're comfortable enough to wear his shirt, he eats cereal from your cabinet, you hung his son's artwork on your refrigerator and you're letting Parker *park it* in your garage on a regular basis."

"Okay, the double meaning was loud and clear that time."

Charlotte leaned forward. "The guy makes you smile."

"It's just a fling." Yet she sounded a smidgen unsure. "You know how these things are—hot at first but they fizzle out."

"What if they don't? If this thing you didn't expect and

can't really control morphs into something bigger than a fling…how do you give it up?"

Understanding blossomed on her friend's face. "You and Nate."

Charlotte nodded and the truth—about Nate, about Tre-Shawn, about the heated talk with her sister and parents—came gushing out. When she finished, she was close to crying but prided herself on the fact that the tears wouldn't fall.

"Can Nate Franco be trusted? Don't answer that with your heart, Lottie. Answer with your brain. Your logic. Being with a man like that in a situation such as this means you have to keep your eyes wide-open."

"And my heart on lockdown, right?"

"Yes," Joey said bluntly. "I don't want you to get hurt. What's happening with TreShawn Dibbs is just a preview of what will go down if Marshall and Tem find out Nate Franco's scratching your itch. More important, Lottie, a heart that loves to its fullest will for damn sure hurt the worst once it's broken."

"Who said anything about love?"

"Love is that fling that won't fizzle…that thing you can't control." Joey set her half-full cereal bowl on the coffee table. "The sooner a *chica* recognizes the warning signs, the better chance she has of saving herself from it."

Love was also a dare that even Charlotte doubted she could take on triumphantly. But as she left her friend's place and let the Fiat's GPS guide her to the address Nate had texted to her, she wasn't sure that she'd ever want to be saved from it. More like saved *by* it. She imagined that love was warmer than fuzzy slippers, more exciting than a sweet kiss, stronger than any forces that tried to get in the way.

Yeah, right.

Charlotte's laugh was dry as she hooked a left onto South Rampart Boulevard. The beautiful Mediterranean architecture of Tivoli Village had her slowing just a bit to admire the view before she turned right onto Alta Drive. The residential towers of exclusive One Queensridge Place pierced the star-dusted sky and rained golden light onto the streets below.

So, Nate's hideout was a castle in the sky. Hers was a running trail roughly an hour away from her family. Like her, he depended on a sanctuary that distanced him from his family—the people he cared about and was so loyal to.

Nate met her in the great room. It had taken her all of three seconds to walk into the luxury lounge and spot him among the guests who were unwinding over drinks and billiards.

In black slacks and a dark blue Dolce & Gabbana shirt with the sleeves pushed up, the man was an invitation to the perfect sin.

He didn't touch her until they were in the private confines of his lavish condo, on the terrace that treated them to a panorama of the city's late-night glimmer. Expecting a kiss, one full of heat and urgency because their time together always seemed so limited, she was startled when he snaked his arms around her waist and pulled her into a hug.

Her feet were still on the ground, but she felt boneless, weightless. Cared for.

"Your folks shouldn't have come at you like a firing squad," he said, withdrawing to search her face with an expression of compassion and empathy.

My heart doesn't care that you're a Franco. Too bad she couldn't trust her heart to govern her life. In past relationships she'd given until she could give no more, but none of those guys had her back when it counted. So her heart was on lockdown, out of the equation, for her own good.

"The owners' priority will always be the team," she said carefully.

Nate was too sharp to miss her hesitation and how she'd responded to him the way someone in PR might want to pacify a pesky reporter. "To some people, family is priority."

"It's more complicated than that for the Blues. We're building a legacy."

"I'm familiar with that, Charlotte."

Because it had in the not-so-distant past been *his* legacy. Details like that were what nudged them apart when they wanted to take a chance on getting closer. Late-night hookups and secret phone calls weren't enough, and Charlotte couldn't imagine what could be enough. Rather than burning themselves out, they were adding fuel to the fire. Yet considering the option of making a clean break made her feel raw inside.

Nate escorted her through the spacious condo, which was furnished extravagantly but devoid of many personal touches. At last he pushed open a finely carved door to reveal a master bedroom large enough to have its own sitting area, basin and a four-poster spectacle that was larger than any king-size bed she'd ever seen.

Continuing into the room, he stopped at the foot of the bed and glanced over at the doorway where she stayed put, resting against the frame. "This is my hideout, and we're off the record here." As his words wrapped around her, he tugged loose his belt while stepping out of his shoes. "I want you to be comfortable with what we say to each other—" he rid himself of his socks, shirt and pants "—what we do..."

Charlotte's breath thinned as he dropped his wristwatch onto the scatter of clothes and went for his boxer briefs. The idea of seeing him totally bare, with all the lights glowing, seemed new to her. Their time together over the past few weeks had all been forbidden and had deprived her of the opportunity to memorize his bronze skin, the cuts and angles of his muscles, the contours of his hands. "What else?"

Pausing long enough to make her wonder whether he'd heard her whisper, he said, "What we want." And he removed the final garment in a motion that had his biceps bunching and thigh muscles tightening.

Nate lowered onto the mattress, piled high with deep-colored linens. Brazen, she looked her fill, then left her high-heeled sandals at the door and crossed the room to him. Unable to touch him everywhere all at once, she settled for stepping between his legs and stroking her fingers over his jaw and through his dark burr-cut hair. "I like your hideout."

"I like this lace on you." His palms roamed the fabric, then sent the flared skirt of the dress billowing up to her hips as he felt his way to her undies. Down they went, and he murmured, "Charlotte, you deserve to know what it feels like to be put first."

Her mind, clouded with the sensations short-circuiting her system, couldn't seem to catch up when Nate sprang to his feet and nudged her backward onto the softness of his ginormous bed.

The lace of her dress flirted with her thighs, blocking her view. There was the vaulted ceiling high above, the scent of spice and citrus around her, and the sounds of his muttered promises tattooing her eardrums. Then there was pressure—delightful and a little scary—of his fingertips drawing her legs up.

The room's crisp coolness caressed her center, only to be replaced with the sensation of warm, wet velvet.... Then he kissed her.

Charlotte jolted, grappled for something. Her leather jacket was littered with zippers that felt cold to the touch. The linens were too silky and she might claw right through them if he continued to feast on her this way.

As she arched up at the intensity of his lips and graze of his teeth, his name fell from her mouth. When his hand gripped her dress where it bunched across her stomach, she grabbed his wrist with both hands, shutting her eyes and closing herself off to everything but feeling and sound… until pleasure broke free.

In moments, he was covering her, pushing the jacket off her shoulders. "There's no one here but us."

The dress followed, in a blur of beige lace launched across the room. "Nothing to think about but this."

"Nate." Eyes open, she let go of all caution. "I want you."

He reached into a nightstand drawer, plucked out a condom and eased back onto the pillows. "Show me."

Charlotte straddled him, rearing forward to clasp the back of his head and fit her mouth to his. In answer he curved his hands possessively over her breasts, grinned when she threw her head back and sank her teeth into her bottom lip.

Navigating his sweat-slicked taut abdomen, Charlotte held his gaze as her fingers danced past his navel to his crotch. His flesh was hard yet the skin was soft as silk, so powerful yet hers for the taking with fingers and lips and tongue. When she settled onto him, anchoring her body to his, she saw in his eyes a man who would love her if she let him.

"You can take back what you said earlier."

Hours later, Charlotte was too sated to leave Nate's bed. Plied with an exotic martini and the freshest damn peach she'd tasted all summer, she let herself be a little lazy on that big soft mattress. Their conversation had drifted to work and he'd shared with her stories about his own experience wading through media lies and working for a team that was owned by a relative. His honesty had comforted her. Now she lay on her belly, naked except for a sheet that tangled around her legs and barely covered her booty.

Bracing his weight on his forearm, Nate hovered over her and leaned in to whisper, "Did you hear me?"

"Mmm-hmm. But why take back the truth?" She closed her eyes against the dark empty sky outside the room's large windows. "I want you. How do you feel about that?"

"Fantastic, 'cause I want you, too." He kissed her between the shoulder blades. "Devastated, 'cause I can't have you."

"Franco versus Blue. Family loyalty. Careers."

He tensed, then murmured, "I'm repaying a debt to my brother."

Charlotte's eyes opened but she didn't dare move for fear of triggering him to shut down and shut her out.

"The bulk of that legacy your family is building was supposed to go to Santino. He lost his career, his woman and his inheritance. It was like someone had come along and knocked down everything good in his life like dominoes."

"No, not everything. He still has your father and you."

"Dad's not the man he used to be—hasn't been for some time. As for me, it's my mission to do something to save the man who saved my life. Charlotte, remember the kids at the benefit? Growing up, I was like them. And I was given hell for it. My mother was proud, but it's always been my father's opinion that matters most. He overlooked me and concentrated on the son with the star quality."

"And Santino? How'd he treat you?"

Nate sighed but answered her. "Santino was a good brother. Fair. Laid-back. A fun guy to be around."

Charlotte's thoughts drifted back to the night at the Di-Gorgio Royal Casino. She'd been shocked to see Santino Franco's intense seriousness in just one glimpse, and for a short moment she'd wondered how handsome he'd be if only he would smile.

"When I was fifteen I didn't want to be a science freak. Neither did Lamont, my best friend at the time. We wanted a way out of being the bottom-feeders at school." His hand stilled on her back. "Lamont told me that a guy had offered him a way out, that I should get in on it. He was in a gang."

Shit. The grief that cut into his voice told her something had gone horribly wrong.

"We were supposed to meet this guy and his boys. But Santino found out, cornered me at home and provoked me until I put my fist in his face. I broke his nose. After we got back from the hospital, we were grounded." He cleared his throat, swore. "Lamont had said he wouldn't go without me, but he went anyway and ended up rolling with that gang. Few months later he was murdered. Bastards from a rival gang tied his shoelaces together and hung his shoes over a power line."

Charlotte gasped. "I thought the shoe tossing was an urban myth."

"Not entirely." He squeezed her shoulder. "I got to live, figured myself to be the luckiest nerd in Las Vegas. Later I was given a choice. Either earn a doctorate in kinesiology and sports medicine, like I'd planned to do, or train guys on my father's team. It was a simple choice. I got what I wanted. Mostly."

Nate had found his own brand of fame in the NFL, and Charlotte didn't doubt that it had shaped who he'd become. But if gaining his father's approval and resolving a debt he thought he owed to his brother were what was driving him, then he had bigger problems than his runaway-train relationship with her. "I'm sorry."

"It happened a long time ago."

"But it did happen. And it's still with you."

"That kind of thing doesn't come up in everyday conversation. But telling you about it felt right."

It did feel right. Sharing deeply hidden truths, discovering intangible closeness. It terrified and thrilled her in equal measures.

"Let's try something," he said, changing the subject as he ran a hand down her spine. "With my finger I'm going to spell out a message on your back. Focus."

She tried. But at the first stroke she erupted in giggles. He tried again but she wriggled away, giggling harder. "I'm ticklish."

"Who's ticklish on their *back?*"

"I am!"

Nate was silent, considering. Then he sat up and flipped her onto her backside as if she weighed nothing. She squeezed her eyes shut in concentration as he stroked a finger over her belly. There was something extraordinarily hot about being naked and unable to see how he was touching her.

"M-I-N-E," she spelled once he'd finished. *Mine.*

Somehow, someway, she wanted to make it true. Opening her eyes to see the stirrings of daybreak rising outside the windows, Charlotte reached up and hauled him into a kiss. For the first time in a long time she wouldn't be running to her hideout in Mount Charleston as the sun rose.

She planned to stay in bed.

Chapter 12

Time fell away, tumbling like the severed bits of shrubbery left in the wake of Bindi's topiary shears. Minutes shifted into hours as she trimmed the first in a row of modest spiral trees that stood at attention like foot soldiers on either side of the Francos' front door. It had passed perfection a while ago, but she couldn't seem to stop obsessing about it and tend to the other trees waiting in line to be groomed.

Besides, if she moved, she would lose vantage of the driveway. When her fiancé finally came home, she wanted the first face he saw to be hers.

Snip.

Last night she'd dressed up in a brand-new dress, practically effervescent with excitement to see a Cirque du Soleil show with her man. But after a half hour crept by with no response to her WHERE R U? texts, he'd responded with CALL YOU BACK but never followed through.

Snip. Snip.

Bindi edged to the side, stepping into the neighboring tree's shade. She rolled her shoulders to relieve the stiffness that had settled there overnight as she slept slumped on a bench in Al's foyer, waiting for him. This morning she'd woken up irritable and had followed a trail of whispers to the kitchen, where the housekeeper, Nadia, entertained the part-time cleaning staff with gossip. At the master of the house's request, while Bindi slept, Nadia had discreetly dropped off his shaving kit and a change of clothes to a hotel in Las Vegas.

Snip!

A chunk of delicate branches and rich green leaves hit the ground at Bindi's feet. She stared at the destruction. It was ruined. The topiary, her engagement, her plans...

She dumped the shears into a wheelbarrow and wiped her quavering hands on the front of her sundress, wanting to berate herself for wasting time she didn't have.

The producer who'd dangled in front of her the big break she'd been dreaming about was losing interest in her reality TV show. The concept was solid and she was attractive enough, but her fiancé didn't have an NFL team anymore and Bindi didn't have much of an engagement. Oh, and at the age of twenty-nine, she had only a few years of *marketability* left.

Visions of red-carpet events, of using communications skills from her unfinished hitch in college to branch out to networks like E! or MTV, of showing her parents that losing their financial and emotional support hadn't broken her, burst like bubbles.

Her phone chirped within her dress's pocket and she glared at Toya Messa's number on the display. As far as friends went, she was down to just Toya, who was weeks away from a fat divorce settlement that would set her for life.

The lucky bitch. Bindi pushed away from the shelter of the trees, ignoring the call and wishing she could ignore the tears that burned hotter than the summer sunshine.

How could she have let a man get the best of her again? No, she hadn't given Al Franco her body. But she'd given him her trust, trust that he'd let slip through his fingers along with the Las Vegas Slayers.

Bindi had lost her leverage, risked her future. Entire nights away from the mansion meant Al wasn't spending those nights alone, wanting her. She wasn't naive; of course withholding was a gamble. But she'd hoped that he would stay true to his word and remain faithful to her for the duration of their engagement. All he'd had to do was show some integrity, marry her and make good on his promise.

I'm going to help you, Bindi, as long as you need me to. You'll have the money you need to take care of yourself. You'll never again have to sell yourself out for an old man like me. You deserve better.

His word had meant nothing. Neither had his son Nate's. At first Nate had wanted to take the necessary measures to get the team back. Something…*someone*…had changed his mind.

The almost seductive growl of a car engine interrupted her bawl-fest, and Bindi clumsily dabbed at her wet eyes. When Al quieted his Porsche 918 Spyder in the driveway and got out clean shaven, wearing sunglasses and a suit different from the one she'd last seen him in, she was there to meet him. From head to toe he looked like a man who'd spent the night in comfort.

"Trimming, were you?" Al pointed his car key toward the spiral trees. "Let's have a look."

Bindi trailed him in silence across the lush lawn, watched him perform a cursory scan. Noticing the damage done to the first topiary, he turned to her for explanation. "You're crying." He shrugged, nudged her chin up gently. "It'll grow back. It's a temporary ugly."

"I waited for you last night, Al."

Al's hand dropped. "Time got away from me. I'm sorry."

"Don't treat me like this. You lie as if you think I'm dumb enough to believe it. You keep me on hold, give me less respect than you do the household staff."

Al frowned at the animosity that shook her voice. "I'm providing for you."

"A car and a few credit cards aren't enough. I have plans for my life. You're going to be my husband."

"A wedding was reasonable before things got out of control, out of my hands."

"What things?"

"Never mind. You want the Lamborghini? It's yours. Take the clothes, too."

"No!" She wasn't some game-show contestant who could be pacified with a few consolation prizes. "What about the reality TV show? Chances like this don't just fall into a woman's lap. Without this shot, I'm sunk. No one wants me."

"That can't be my problem anymore." Al reached for her engagement ring, but she jerked away. "Take some time to come to terms." Then he strode to his car and was gone again.

Bindi twisted the ring on her finger, almost shivering with panic. The tears reemerged, bringing up an angry sob from someplace down deep. She lunged for the nearest tree, gripping handfuls and yanking. Branches snapped and the tree quivered, but she couldn't dislodge it from the ground. When her hands slipped, she staggered backward. What she'd put into this house was more deeply rooted than she'd thought.

"Bindi."

She twisted around to find Santino at the top of the front steps, his tattooed arms crossed. He stood motionless but watchful, like a hawk considering its prey. Great. If he hadn't seen what had just happened, surely he'd heard every mortifying word of it.

Not that she was obligated to acknowledge it—or the man surveying her now. If she could just hold it together long enough to get inside the mansion, she could pretend, for a while, that her fiancé hadn't dumped her on the front lawn.

With tearstains and dirty hands, she took the steps swiftly. But at the precise moment that she put up a hand to warn him against speaking to her, Santino stopped her with a loose grip on her wrist.

She straightened to her full height, looking him square in the face through her tears. True, she wasn't a football warrior as he'd been not so long ago. But she was tough in other ways. And nothing could crush her fighting spirit. At the end of the day, it was all that remained.

"Sounds like he's done." Santino inclined his head, his dark hair brushing his shoulders. "Whatever deal you had going with him—it's over."

"Cute, how you seem to think you have a say in *my* relationship."

"You mean the relationship that was a damn joke from the get-go? The one he ended just now? Yeah, *that* relationship." His gaze followed a tear that trickled freely when she blinked, and his features seemed to tighten into a frown. "Walk away, Bindi."

"Don't break out the celebratory champagne yet." He didn't appear to be in a particularly celebratory mood, yet she never could gauge whether anything but resentment lived inside him. She flashed the engagement ring. "As long as I have this, I'm still in the picture."

Fueled with desperation, she escaped to the guest room she'd chosen upon moving in, grabbed her cell phone and committed to a decision without giving herself the chance to change her mind. Then, tossing the phone aside, she sank to the bed. Guilt, something she didn't know she could still feel, swamped her.

It had taken a few phone calls, and more cash than she'd wanted to spend, to find dirt on Charlotte Blue once she'd gotten an idea of what to search for. It had taken one night of following Nate to catch him in a rendezvous with the woman and figure out why he'd defected to Charlotte's side.

Bindi had no loyalty to Charlotte or Nate or anyone else, yet she'd hesitated all the same. Now it was make it or break it, and she'd had only one real choice.

To save herself.

With Slayers Stadium in the final stages of its renovation, the perimeter of the place was crammed with trucks ranging from ordinary pickups to cherry pickers to cranes. If the building was Marshall and Tem's oyster, then the owners' suite was the pearl.

As one of the many assistants ushered Charlotte inside, she was excited to get her first look at the refreshed space. Since being persuaded to distance herself from TreShawn Dibbs, who had taken it personally just as she'd known he would, Charlotte had been at best cordial to Danica and their parents. It was past time to squash the tension between them. When her father had texted her at the top of the morning, summoning her from Mount Charleston for a long lunch at the stadium, she'd felt optimistic about finally putting all the hurt feelings and disappointment aside.

The details of the luxury suite stood out all at once: Parisian-influenced furniture, a wet bar, glass panels that showcased the heart of the stadium. Charlotte's favorite spot in the whole place—the field—was a mess. Would it be presentable, functional, for the next at-home exhibition game?

"We're on schedule," Tem said, sweeping into the room with her tablet. "The turf has taken well and the painting crew will be here at five sharp tomorrow morning to make over the seats."

"You read my mind, Ma." Charlotte reached out to hug Tem but grasped the air as her mother breezed past to set the tablet on the bar.

"Then it's nice to be tuned in to my daughters every once in a while. You accused me of not knowing Martha, and it was infuriating because your father and I like to think we know Martha, Danica and you quite well—as parents ought to. But it turns out we don't. You, for example. We knew you were stubborn, defiant. We didn't know you were so reckless."

"What does that mean?" Charlotte's skin prickled as Tem picked up the tablet and joined her at the glass panels. "Is this a bad time to have come? Pop invited me."

"Marshall and your sisters will be here shortly. You'll know everything then."

"That sounds ominous."

Tem said nothing more until Danica and Martha entered the suite, followed by Marshall…who had whipped out a bottle of antacids.

Charlotte was beginning to suspect she had too many secrets. She cleared her throat. "We haven't all sat down to lunch together in months."

"Getting our franchise in good shape is paramount, Lottie." This from her father. "We've been busy blocking problem after problem. Tem."

Tem swiped her finger across the tablet, tapped the

screen and handed the device to Charlotte. "This is one of those problems."

Charlotte stared at the tablet, at the image of her younger self. Naked except for a pair of thigh-high athletic socks and a cleverly placed champion belt, she looked into the camera through a forest of straight teased hair. There was attitude in her eyes.

Attitude, and purpose, had propelled her to pose for a risqué magazine that she'd assumed was defunct by now. Twelve years ago, when the photo had been taken, the magazine had been something underground and not even close to the popularity of *Playboy* or *Penthouse*. The payment she'd received had been enough to fund the summer Eat & Run program in New England, combining nutrition education and marathon training, she'd wanted to participate in. In college on her parents' dime, she'd had to comply with their suggestions—demands—because the threat of them cutting her off hung over her head. That summer they'd wanted her home and had refused to pay for the program. So she'd found her own way, had agreed to straighten her hair to amplify her look and posed for a few clicks of a camera.

After her next visit home she had felt ashamed, and in an attempt to wipe the slate clean, she'd had her hair cut short. Then she'd put the transgression behind her.

But it had come back, on some celebrity gossip website. How? She'd told no one—not even her college roommate, Krissy O'Claire, who had been studying abroad that summer—about the photos. Charlotte's guilt trip hadn't allowed her to buy a copy of the magazine for herself. She'd never even known until now which pose had been used.

"Our attorney is on this, Lottie," Martha said. "He's

having the pic taken off the website. How old were you when you did this?"

"Twenty."

"You weren't underage. That's a good thing, isn't it?" Martha looked to Danica, then their parents. "And at least her lady parts are covered." She bopped over to peer at the tablet. "Somewhat."

"Seems you've had more Charlotte Slipups than we know about," Tem said. "You had a duty to this franchise to warn us about something of this nature. You're on probation till the start of the season. But tell me why. Why didn't you consider how this would affect your future?"

"I did it *for* my future. You and Pop cut me off the summer I wanted to stay on campus for a fitness program. You didn't believe I'd find my own money to pay for it, but I did. I took the dare."

Danica crossed her arms. "God, Lottie, you can't take dares like that."

"Danni, can't you see she's upset enough?" Martha said. "Lottie, the publicity department is trying to minimize the damage. We'll need to prep your statement and release that. There's going to be some debate on ESPN, you can count on that. After the Dibbs issue, people are sort of supersensitive to your mistakes. They're second-guessing you as a role model for young girls interested in male-dominated sports."

"It was never about becoming a role model," Charlotte said. "Not for me. I'm sorry if that makes me look selfish, but it's always been about sports. The game. The role-model thing is something that y'all were capitalizing on. Can we all be honest enough to admit it?"

"Damn it, Charlotte. This should humble you!" The boom of Marshall's voice seemed powerful enough to fell an entire forest.

"You mean subdue me?" Charlotte handed the tablet to her mother. "It hasn't. Like Martha said, it's upset me. I don't know who could've leaked this."

"Chaz Lakan called me this morning," Tem said. "A woman he said is acquainted with you contacted him for information. She said you'd mentioned to her that you hit a rough patch in college. He didn't know what her angle was until now."

Charlotte hadn't mentioned her college blunder to anyone…except Nate. "The woman. What's her name?"

"Bindi Paxton. She's engaged to Alessandro Franco."

The weight of the truth hit her hard, knocked the breath out of her even as she stood totally still with the eyes of her family centered on her. What she'd told Nate had ended up in the hands of his father's fiancée and had then ended up in cyberspace. Coincidental or deliberate?

Coincidental, my ass. Charlotte started to rush out of the suite, but her mother's grip on her arm tugged her back.

"Lottie, do you have no care about your image or your family?"

More like my family's image. "Ma, I'm sorry that what I do and who I am hurts you. But you, and everyone else, need to consider that this photo is just as provocative as what shows up in magazines like *GQ* and *Sports Illustrated*. You're a product of the beauty-pageant circuit. Tell us how many times you were judged on how attractive you were in a bathing suit." At that her mother let her go and Charlotte kept walking. "I regret that a photo taken twelve years ago can start up a firestorm, but I'm also glad that I finally saw it. The woman in that photo is okay with herself. Fierce. Unafraid. I miss her."

Charlotte marched out of the suite with Martha in close pursuit.

"Wait, Lottie!" Martha flung her arms around Charlotte, squeezing even as Charlotte's arms remained loose at her sides. "What are you going to do?"

"Go back to camp. There are things that need to be done." *And people who need to be set straight.*

Charlotte made it back to Desert Luck as the coaching staff was dispersing from a meeting and the players were gearing up for the second two-a-day. Glances. Frowns. Stares. Chuckles. They were all directed at her as she strode through the facility to the staff lounge. It was as if she'd shown up naked.

In a way she had. There were more tablets, phones and computers in this place than an electronics store. In the age of internet, Facebook and Twitter, all it took was one person to forward a link. It was too bad that a single long-ago impulsive photo shoot could throw her plans, career, *image* into a vortex.

What was worse? She didn't entirely hate that she'd stripped down in front of a camera. The experience had been challenging, frightening and liberating all at once. What she did hate was that she'd tried to sweep it under the rug rather than embrace and own it. She hated that she'd given Bindi Paxton—and Nate Franco—the power to use her secret against her in some sort of revenge play.

Nate. There he was, in a talk with Kip and Whittaker near the lounge's kitchenette. As she went to her locker, she heard their quarterback's name and exhaled in relief. It was refreshing that not everyone was distracted to stupidity about an old-as-dirt naked photo.

"Charlotte, a word?"

Turning, she saw Kip advancing toward her and cast a narrowed-eyed glance beyond his shoulder at Nate. "Coach." Kip proffered a cold bottle of Evian, which she accepted with a nod of thanks. It didn't matter if you were thirsty or not. If your coach offered you a water, you took it. "What's the update on Brock's shoulder?"

"Rehab therapy's going good. Backup QB's set for the rest of preseason. Then Brock will play game one. He wants to play. I trust him to know his body." A beat later he said, "Word of the day is *Charlotte*."

"Considering it could be *boobies,* I'm okay with that." The sarcasm was met with a look of concern. "It won't stop me from doing my job. Does it bother you?"

Kip's face split into an uncomfortable half grimace, half laugh. "It's sports. A woman's physique shouldn't matter so much, but our players are focusing more on your picture than they're focusing on handling the damn football."

"Sounds more like a conversation you should have with them, Coach."

Kip took a moment to consider. "I trust you to know yourself and what you can handle." He clapped a hand to her shoulder, then eyed his watch. "Need you on the sidelines in fifteen."

Grabbing a cotton tee and shorts from her duffel gave her comfort. What if she was no longer a part of this team, no longer welcome into this lounge and the lives of the young men whose overall well-being was as important to her as her own? She was supposed to be better than perfect. In the eyes of her parents, she'd already fallen short. Training camp was meant to weed out the weak.

So would she be among those cut when the team finalized its roster?

The click of the door's lock engaging had her turning to see that she was now alone in the lounge with Nate.

"Really, Nate? It's fine to spill my secrets to Bindi Paxton, but let's keep the door locked on yours?" When he made no move to open the door, she shrugged and yanked off the street clothes she'd worn to the stadium.

Heat flared in his eyes and she stiffened. What part of him…their relationship…had been a lie? Was the attraction tumbling through her, even as she cursed the moment she agreed to join Joey for drinks at VooDoo, authentic?

"The general public has seen everything you've seen," she gritted out, stepping into her mesh athletic shorts.

"Not everything, Charlotte. They haven't seen where I touched you to make you break apart in my arms."

Even then you were lying to me. "Guess that makes you special, huh?" She faced her locker and finished dressing, feeling his attention on her all the while.

"We have to talk about this, Charlotte."

"Gloat or apologize—it's all the same. Either way we're through."

"Does the front office know about us?"

"No, Nate. Sabotage is *your* thing. It actually didn't occur to me to retaliate." *Don't shake. Don't show him that you fooled yourself and fell in love with him.* "Targeting me. Was this to avenge some wrongdoing you think my father committed against yours? Or was this about me?"

"Both, at first. It killed to know your family stole this team from mine, that your folks could fire me on a whim. I was going out of my mind trying to make things right."

"Why go after me? What did *I* do?" Charlotte stopped. "Wait…I was your weapon. You wanted to get to my family through me. But you don't get it, even now. I'm not the Blues' Achilles' heel. When you hurt me, *I'm* the only one who's hurt."

"Bindi didn't tell me what she was planning."

"Weren't you plotting with her?"

"Yes—*at first*. After a while I was done with it."

"Why?"

"It got out of hand! I wasn't supposed to love—" Nate swore, kneaded his forehead with his fingertips. "The magazine photo? I had no idea it existed until I got here today and found some of the boys passing around a phone."

Charlotte shifted her weight to keep from falling into her nervous habit. "I heard what you didn't say, Nate. And I hope this got so out of hand that you ended up hurting yourself. It wouldn't have worked out for us anyway. Great sex can't change who we are." She shut her locker. "Coach is expecting us. You go first."

She waited ten minutes—long enough to dab away the tears that had caught her by surprise the moment Nate left the room—before putting on her sunglasses and marching out.

"Charlotte, hold up." Royce Davis, the wide-receivers coach, sprinted the short distance to where she stood outside the staff lounge.

"Royce." Drained from her conversation with Nate, she was anxious to get outside and start sweating out the heartache. Work was the salve she needed. It could distract her, tire her out, consume her. The only thing it wouldn't do was make her forget. "Can we walk and talk? I need to be out there."

"After you."

With him trailing her she waited several beats for him to get to it, but at his continued silence she threw a glance over his shoulder to see his gaze attached to her backside. "What do you want?"

"Charlotte," he said on a low chuckle, "I can answer that with words or with action."

To illustrate, he gave her butt a punishing squeeze and went for the waistband of her shorts. She promptly ripped his hand away and pinned it to his chest. "Try this again and you'll answer to Coach, with words, why I broke your wrist."

Royce shoved away, spitting a derogatory word.

Charlotte went onto the sunny field, straight to Kip, and rose up to say into his ear, "Royce Davis grabbed my ass in the building, tried to take it further. I...talked him out of it. It happened in the hall, so pull the security tape for proof. If you can handle this without involving administration, I'd appreciate not being called into a meeting with my folks again anytime soon."

Flabbergasted at her cool, matter-of-fact demeanor, he asked, "What do you want to do now?"

"D'you have to ask?" She was already jogging backward to the sidelines. "Work."

Chapter 13

The last place Charlotte thought she'd wind up after camp the next evening was on Main Street inside a utilitarian interview room at Las Vegas's Office of Diversion Control.

Chilled, she blew into her hands, rubbed them together for warmth. The air-conditioning was overcompensating for the heat and humidity that hung to the pitch-black night. On top of that, she'd never seen so many cold, impassive faces.

And here she thought *she* worked with a complicated group.

At the late hour Joey managed to look fresh and alert in her snug pantsuit and startlingly blue T-strap Saint Laurent shoes. She was working her first controlled-pharmaceuticals case, which was the biggest assignment she'd sunk her teeth into since her transfer to Las Vegas. It called for late hours, long days and total focus. Which meant personal ties took a backseat. In light of this, Joey's inviting Charlotte to this location at this time of night was two kinds of strange.

When she entered the interview room carrying two cups of hot brew in one hand—both for herself, as Charlotte was still nursing the foam cup of lukewarm water-cooler H2O another agent had offered—she took the chair beside Charlotte and set her cane across her lap.

The gesture took off some of the interrogation edge, but not much. Joey rested her arms on the table, steepled her manicured fingers. "Use evidence for maximum results. It's a cardinal rule, for me at least."

"Evidence?"

"Nate Franco. Let's say I took a professional look at him." At the admission, Joey toyed with the ID badge clipped to her lapel. "Called in a favor to D.C., kept it need-to-know."

Charlotte held up a hand. "What the hell? I asked you not to do that."

"I had to make a judgment." Pushing back her curly brown hair, Joey took a swallow of coffee. "When I found out you were sleeping with Nate."

"And that was a problem? What are you, a sex narc?"

"Can't you recognize when someone's watching your back?" Joey yanked her badge from her jacket and slapped it onto the table between them. "I'm putting my ass on the line telling you what I found out, warning you about who you're getting all tangled up with. Nate's another guy with an ulterior motive. Like Wade."

"Nate's not just another Wade. I didn't love Wade."

"And there it is." Joey waited long enough for Charlotte to understand the magnitude of her own words. "You invest too much of yourself into relationships."

"Maybe. But it's better than holding back. I know part of the reason you took this pharmaceuticals case is to distance yourself from Parker. You're afraid he'll mess you over, like that black-ops guy did. Well, Jo, Nate isn't Parker and I'm not you. I trust and I love, and I get my heart broken. It's not your duty to save me from your mistakes."

"Fine." But it wasn't. A nerve had been hit. "I took a look, had D.C. check my homework. Nate is clean. It's his father who's in deep—a gambling network living and breathing in the DiGorgio. We've only scratched the surface, but this is what I can tell you. Before he sold the team, Franco was using a proxy to bet on Slayers games. He manipulated the outcomes of those games."

"How?"

"A bounty. Incentives. Bonuses. Under-the-table payments to his coaching staff. A few still work for the team— assistant offensive-line coach, wide-receivers coach. All it took was the right players to cooperate, particularly his offensive men. Alessandro Franco took a huge financial loss, and the next Sunday his son got the living hell knocked out of him in a game against—"

Charlotte knew her eyes were wide as saucers. It was unbelievable and yet made perfect sense. "The Slayers."

Joey nodded. "That week Franco needed his team to win to try to dig himself out. Santino was so good of a player that he was a threat, so he had to be stopped. The erratic wins and losses, the tackle that killed his son's career, the sale of a relatively lucrative franchise, lying about Marshall intimidating him? The man was covering his ass." She nudged Charlotte gently with an elbow. "What will you do with this information?"

"Nate and I had an agreement—no cheap shots." Her friend gave her a meaningful look that said, *Wouldn't leaking a nudie pic of you be considered a cheap shot?* She stood to leave. "Maximum results, huh?"

Another nod. "You know what I'd do. But you're not

me. Just know that I can't *un*know what I found out. Cor-
ruption like this can't be ignored. A man lost his career…
could've lost his life." Joey stood with her cane, pulled
Charlotte into a hug. "*Dios.* We've both got issues, you
know that, right?"

"Must be why we're such good friends."

Revenge was a dance. A tango of attack and retaliate. Charlotte wasn't much of a dancer, though. When
she found her escort behind the velvet rope leading to the
front entrance of DiGorgio Royal Casino, where an Italian
opera sensation would be performing for the city's elite,
she didn't have revenge in mind.

What she *did* have was backup in the form of a jaded
quarterback who had the looks and scandalous reputation
of a Hollywood prince and nothing to lose. Dex Harper
had harbored suspicions all along, but no one—including
Charlotte—had been willing to listen. What he'd claimed
was a team conspiracy and a corporate screw-over, the
public had perceived as his attempt to escape responsibility for his own underperformance and shitty leadership.
His release from the Slayers upon the change of ownership
hadn't been unexpected—more like anticipated. Now, with
no contract and no credibility, Dex was fired up enough to
talk to anyone who might hold the clout to clear his name.

Charlotte found Dex among the stream of well-dressed
guests bleeding into the casino. He greeted her with a short
nod. A pair of aviator sunglasses shielded his eyes. "If Nate
has us thrown out—"

"I don't think he will." Nate may have quit trying to
plead his case and draw her into conversation at camp, but
when she'd suggested they talk tonight, in person, he'd
named the time and place without hesitation. What he
didn't know was that she'd be walking into the casino with

Dex. "But if he does, then I'll try again. I'll keep trying until I get through to him. We're giving him the chance to get ahead of the avalanche before the league comes down on his father."

With no time or inclination to plot, Charlotte had chosen to bring her evidence to Nate first. She'd toyed with the idea of saying nothing until the commissioner's office made a move against Al. But Nate needed to know the truth before the media captured it, shaped it, exploited it.

Charlotte's skin prickled with awareness as her gaze settled on Nate, who sat at a table in the Mahogany Lounge, his features serious.

As the mezzo-soprano's haunting aria drifted from the casino ballroom, Charlotte approached Nate, with her companion following close. "Dex," she said, turning to him, "give me a minute?"

"I can give you as long as it takes me to finish a beer. After that, I start talking. And if Franco won't listen, then I'll find someone who will." The man shrugged in a take-it-or-leave-it gesture and cut a path toward the far end of the bar.

Nate's gaze cruised her boldly, intimately, as she closed the distance between them. "For days I've been trying to get time with you, Charlotte, and when I finally do, you bring him." He jerked his head in the direction Dex had gone. "Didn't know you and Harper were a packaged deal."

"Probably because we're not." Charlotte didn't want more walls between them, more obstacles to get in the way of her shedding light on the truth. "Nate, he was telling the truth. The team—your father—set him up to fail."

"Thought sabotage wasn't your thing. You're a Blue and you're above that, right? So how are you gonna turn around and come at me with this?"

"I'm coming at you with what the FBI considers the

truth," she whispered. "Dex was set up, and it was all under your father's orders. Al offered a bounty. He paid his boys to injure opponents and to piss on their quarterback's plays."

Dex approached, and though Nate appeared furious enough to overturn the table, he let the man take a seat and have his say.

Charlotte wasn't immune to empathy or whatever emotion compelled her to come within inches of covering his hand with hers, wrapping her arms around him, promising to wait for him to emerge from what hell would come. As Dex recounted hearing players say "Payday!" to the teammate who had with a hard tackle sent Santino Franco off the field on a cart, Charlotte retreated.

"I gotta go." She rushed out of the Mahogany Lounge, moving quickly and zigzagging through so many clusters of guests that she lost her way and sought the nearest exit.

And was confronted with an alleyway, which meant the parking garage was on the opposite side. She'd go in later, pick her way to the valet, claim her vehicle and escape. At least out in the open, surrounded by battered asphalt, she could breathe and try to wash away the memory of the wrath in Nate's expression as Dex's words registered and Nate realized that his father had paid for the illegal play that had ruined Santino's NFL career.

Navigating the concrete steps, Charlotte gripped the rusted handrail and gulped in a breath of the night air. As the thick glass door swung open, she turned and was face-to-face with Nate.

"I'm leaving," she said, sparing him from ordering her off the premises. "If coming here with Dex seems like an ambush, then okay. I can't be sorry for that."

She hadn't meant to touch him, but he made a move to go left and she went right, and she lost her sense at the moment of contact. One of his hands twisted her hair, bringing her face to his. The other settled on her hip, squeezing, imprinting, as he drew her down the last two steps.

Charlotte hooked herself to him, taking what his kiss offered until they hit the wall and reality invaded. Easing away, she sank to one of the steps with no regard to the pristine elegance of her dress.

"Why didn't you go to the front office? The commissioner?" Nate asked.

"I know what it's like to be blindsided." She rose to her feet, pulled open the door. "And it's time we both take a look at where our loyalties lie."

Nate went straight to his father's Lake Las Vegas mansion, but he had zero recall of the drive. There was only the concentrated anger that had saturated him since the revelation about his father's deception took hold. Even without indisputable evidence in front of him, he knew that Dex Harper and Charlotte had been laying down the truth. And you just don't ignore what makes too damn much sense.

Hooking a turn into the driveway, he saw his brother advancing to his own sports car. He flashed his high beams, got out and said to Santino, "Don't take off. I need to talk to Dad…and you need to be there when I do."

The men trooped into the house. Al sat alone in the extravagant game room, at the custom-built poker table with chips, cards and a bottle of port at his fingertips. At Nate's terse "I have business with you, Dad," Al flicked a glance his way. Upon catching the simmering fury Nate couldn't mask, the man fished a cigar from his jacket pocket.

"Business with me. Then why is he here?" Al pointed the cigar at Santino.

Nate approached the poker table. "Damn it, Dad. I

know, all right? *I know.* Now Santino's going to know, too. You're going to tell him."

Al slumped against his chair as realization dawned. "Gloria wouldn't have let this happen. She wouldn't have let me hit the bottom." He swore. Then, with his stare fixed on the scatter of cards, he started talking.

At the words "I paid cash for that hit—the one that brought you down, Santino," Santino crossed the room fast and had Al by the collar, hauling him up from his chair. "You wanted a star!" he growled. "I gave you that, and you screwed up my career."

Nate shouldered his way between them, shoving his brother back. "It's not your fight, bro. Not mine. It's Dad's fight, against himself."

"I built my entire life according to *his* fucking blueprints for me, Nate," Santino said coldly. "I lost everything—and that man right there jumped it off."

Nate wouldn't ask his brother to brush off the rage, to ignore the betrayal. "Blame him, then, Santino. But don't be like him. Be better than that."

Al swept up his cigar and made for the door, only to have Bindi block his path.

"I heard everything, Al."

"*Sì?* Hear this. It's over. Be out by morning, and leave the house key."

"We had an agreement. How could you gamble away our future?"

"You were *never* a part of my future," Al seethed, pushing past her.

The devastation on Bindi's face was familiar to Nate. It glinted in his brother's eyes, even now as Santino sought out the minibar.

Nate strode out of the room. He'd let an incredible

woman slip out of his life, all because he'd been chasing someone else's dream—someone else's *blueprints* for him.

His father was right about one thing. It was over.

Cleopatra's Barge was more than a nightclub…more than a Las Vegas tourist attraction with a kick-ass floating craft and no cover charge. It was an inspiration. At least, it was to a woman who constantly fantasized about drifting off to a brand-new life.

Bindi hunkered down on her stool at the bar. She'd better get comfortable—the Franco men had a habit of keeping her waiting or not following through at all with their end of an agreement. And she wouldn't be surprised if Charlotte Blue ignored the message Bindi had left with Desert Luck Center's receptionist.

The bartender knew her by name and Bindi didn't have to ask for the whiskey sour he brought to the end of the bar. She crossed her legs, relishing the way the denim hugged her. She'd missed jeans. Al had preferred her in clothes that showed off her legs.

"Cheers."

"Toasting to waiting again?" Charlotte took the stool beside Bindi. "We've gotta stop meeting like this."

The woman's words were light but there was seriousness and warning in her voice that Bindi didn't want to poke at. "The things I did…the reasons why…were wrong. I'm sorry for setting you up. I had a stake in Al getting the team back and it's all I could think about—even when I'd started to realize his story about your father threatening him was suspect. In the beginning Nate was in it with me, but he backed out. Because of you."

Charlotte watched her in silence.

Well, what had Bindi expected? An "Apology accepted! Let's be BFFs!" and air kisses? She went on and could blame the whiskey for jarring loose words and emotions that should've hardened in her heart long before now. "I fight dirty. It's just how I survive. My parents chopped this apple off the family tree a *long* time ago."

"We're a lot more alike than you know, Bindi. If you'd put on the brakes during your quest to publicly humiliate me out of my career, you might've realized it." Charlotte abandoned her stool while fishing into her purse. "This is yours."

Bindi waved away the pig flashlight. "Keep it. Or at least toss it in the trash when my back's turned. I gave that to you in kindness. I'd like to think I did *something* in kindness."

"Goodbye, Bindi." Key chain in hand, Charlotte left.

Another whiskey later, Bindi swiveled on her stool to see Santino making his way to the bar. "Coffee. Cream, sugar." But when the bartender presented him with a steaming cup of java that looked hot enough to have been brewed in hell, Santino remained standing, as if he had no intent to stay and drink that coffee.

"Give this to Al," she said, removing the engagement ring from her finger. "I don't know if you're speaking to him after what we found out. But he needs to know I sold the dresses and skirts and didn't keep his ring."

"For you." Santino slid the coffee toward her. Then he scooped the engagement ring from her palm. "Done with Las Vegas?"

"I was going to take this city. That was the plan. Instead it took me—hard—and it's not done yet. Investigators are going to want to keep me close to see what I know about Al's extracurricular activities." Bindi cast a glance about the room. "On the upside, I have this place to keep coming back to. I can blend in with the crowd."

"I don't think that's possible."

Cynicism aside, she supposed he was right. In red four-inch heels, skinny jeans and a black lace top, with diamond daggers hanging from her earlobes and her hair pulled back into a neat blond bow, she did sort of stand out.

"Wherever you end up, try doing things differently," he said.

"Follow your own advice."

"My father—the man I idolized—destroyed my career. Everything I was fighting for was a goddamn lie. Yeah, things can't exactly go back to the way they used to be."

"When you put it like that, I guess maybe you're worse off than I am." Shouldn't that fact make her feel even a smidgen better? It didn't, and she felt agitated because of it. Life was simpler when she could view Santino and Nate as adversaries and nothing more.

"Is that all, Bindi?"

"I'm keeping the Lamborghini." With that, she took off in a quick stride, weaving around patrons and servers until she reached the exit—

Where the devil was her purse?

With an annoyed sigh, she revolved slowly, peering back through the packed lounge to where she'd left Santino with that untouched coffee. Except now he was holding up her crocodile coin purse, watching her with an expression that was…amused? No way. The man was too damn serious to crack a smile.

"I'll take that." She reclaimed the accessory with a snatch, then hesitated as she considered the coffee. It was a pool of dark emptiness. It'd chase her whiskey but wouldn't give her prospects or perspective. Even so, she met Santino's eyes, took a healthy swig from the cup, set it down.

And walked away.

Chapter 14

I hope this got so out of hand that you ended up hurting yourself.

Charlotte's words stuck with Nate. Revenge backfired, all right. He knew that now. Somehow he'd gone too far, gotten way too cocky thinking he was resilient against passion that could distract and love that could cut if snatched away too quickly. From the get-go he'd gotten it wrong, because Charlotte Blue had never been his enemy and didn't deserve to be collateral damage of his victory-at-all-costs mission to reverse the sale of an NFL franchise that wasn't, in fact, his be-all and end-all.

As furious as losing claim to the team had made him, Nate was more affected by the betrayal he'd seen in Charlotte's eyes when he'd come clean. By playing her, he'd played himself.

For what? Validation and a pat on the back from a man who'd lost himself to his own weaknesses? Envy and vengeance were part of Al's game. He'd gambled with people's lives, manufactured lies to protect himself.

But in the end Nate was responsible for his own choices. It had been his choice to chase Al's approval, to be loyal to his father and not himself. Now he was choosing to back out of the game.

Nate entered the staff lounge with two confidential letters secured in the interior pocket of his dark Italian blazer. One was a full disclosure addressed to the NFL commissioner; the other a statement of resignation to Marshall and Temperance Blue.

"Where's Kip?" he asked one of the assistant coaches after scanning the room.

"Meeting with Whittaker and Charlotte." The man's sharp stare was fixed on the congregation at Royce Davis's locker.

Nate's instincts had him joining the group in time to hear one of the men gibe, "Those tits, that behind—damn. Ain't sayin' I wouldn't want to tap that, but I'm not dumbass enough to actually do it. I like having a job."

"Hardly touched her, but they got me packing my shit anyway."

"Touched who? Charlotte?" Nate waited, his face void of emotion, his arms loose. But he was ready to within a moment's notice put a fist in Royce's face. His imagination was wild, taunting him with scenes of Royce putting his hands on Charlotte.

"You know it," Royce answered, shoving clothes into a duffel bag. "Should've bent her over when I had the chance."

Nate's hand closed around the man's throat. Royce staggered, caught by surprise as he hit the adjacent locker. The metal rang at the force of impact. If Nate was fined, so be it. Men surged forward, hollering, cursing, pulling at his shoulders.

"We're just talking, aren't we, Royce? We can talk about Charlotte Blue, or we can talk about what I know you did under old management." Just as quickly as he'd gripped the man's throat, he let him go. "Stay away from Charlotte. Touch her again, and I *will* find you."

Royce's eyes turned flinty; his thick lips pressed together in a firm line. But he didn't speak until the other men jostled them apart, and, turning, he saw Kip, Whittaker and Charlotte crowding the doorway.

Charlotte slapped a palm to her forehead. "Really, Nate?"

"He put his hands on you, Charlotte."

"And we were handling it," she said, gesturing to Kip, Whittaker and herself. "It's not your place to step in."

"Franco. Davis. I'm going to need to see you both in my office in five," Kip bellowed. "Get your stuff."

Royce Davis wouldn't be returning to camp—everyone knew that. Nate wouldn't be, either, because his resignation was effective immediately. No one but he knew that yet.

As he was being escorted into the hall, he muttered to Charlotte as he passed, "You may not want me to protect you, but it's what I have to do."

In Kip's office Royce refused to discuss the incident and left without saying a word when the coach finally told him to get the hell out. Then Kip told Nate, "I see things around me that people think I don't. They all might have the impression that you went off on Davis because he put his hands on a woman. I think you went off because he put his hands on *your* woman." Frowning now, he added, "What are you going to do about the situation?"

Nate knew his decision would be met with protest, especially from Kip and Whittaker, who valued his expertise and believed it took not just winning players but a winning staff to claim victory. "I have a document for Marshall and Temperance Blue." He shook Kip's hand. "I wish the Slayers luck."

The Blues kept him waiting for over twenty minutes, during which Nate sat in the reception area turning over and over in his hand the envelope addressed to the owners. With each minute that passed, he felt surer about the contents.

Finally, he was summoned into the office where he'd once been welcome without requiring permission. Another reminder that life had forever changed. This was no longer his family's legacy. The formal investigation into his father's misconduct hadn't yet begun, but there would be no going back to the days in which the Las Vegas Slayers franchise was the Francos' kingdom.

A new era—*dynasty*—had begun.

Marshall sat at a massive glass table, his wife polished and regal at his side. He crooked an eyebrow at the envelope in Nate's hand. "That a formal apology for the hell your family brought on my daughter?"

"No, it's not. But if we're talking about Charlotte, I know for a fact that she's faced every obstacle without you. In spite of you."

"Hold up, now," Marshall began, pushing back his chair. He stood and his size seemed to absorb the room. "Folks on my payroll don't speak to me or my wife like that. Now, Charlotte hasn't made the most…strategic…decisions."

"Sir." Nate lowered his head; the envelope burned his fingers. "This game is only part strategy. The rest is heart. Charlotte's got so much heart that she didn't tell you Royce Davis overstepped with her."

"Davis?" Marshall asked, a note of death in his voice.

"She handled Davis without enlisting your help. There's a reason for that."

"Excuse me," Tem interrupted. "Are you accusing us of leaving her to work through her troubles at camp alone?"

"Ma'am. I didn't say she was alone."

Tem dropped back with a gasp, clutching at her husband's shoulder. "What the—? What is this?"

"This," he said, pointing to himself, "is the man who held her when you shut down the progress she was making with Dibbs. I'm the man who knows she needs more than tough love. I'm the man who screwed up and lost her." He let the letter drop onto the burgundy blotter in front of Marshall. "This—" he jabbed the envelope "—is my resignation."

Nothing *good* could come of being called from Mount Charleston to her parents' luxury suite at the stadium in Las Vegas smack in the middle of a jam-packed training day. That in mind, Charlotte resolved to be calm, reserved and professional with a capital *P*.

A solid plan.

Passing her sisters, who surveyed her as if they detected something different about her but couldn't be sure what, she walked into the owners' suite.

Tem was pacing, wearily rubbing the back of her neck with one hand and gesturing wildly to Marshall. "Charlotte." She stopped as crisply as a soldier at attention. "Why didn't you confide in us about Royce Davis? He resigned, depriving us of the joy of firing his ass."

Hmm. This was no ordinary Temperance Tantrum. Her picture-perfect mother had just said the *ass*-word.

"I handled it. Coach and HR helped me take care of it. Davis cooperated. There was no further incident, no need to drag you and Pop into it." Charlotte smiled encouragingly, crossing the room to touch Tem's shoulder. "Chill, Ma. Who even brought this to you?"

The tension in the room seemed strong enough to shake the foundation they stood on. Tem nudged Charlotte's hand off her shoulder. She twirled and the skirt of her daisy-yellow summer dress floated around her legs. "Tell us, Lottie. If you were to write a 'what I did at summer camp' list, would the name *Nate Franco* appear on it?"

A shuffling sound came from the hall where Danica and Martha waited. Charlotte ignored it. Now she was pissed with a capital *P*. "Oh, it'd top the list."

The daredevil in her couldn't resist the snarky answer, and though Charlotte winced at her parents' shocked expressions, she was blown away to discover...it was true.

Nate had given her a type of friendship she would never find with anyone else, because with him she'd held back nothing even as her career and hunger for her parents' approval hung like an overcast sky.

A sharp bump on the other side of the door had Marshall cutting across the room. The door swung open to reveal Danica and Martha, who'd barely been able to stop themselves from tumbling onto the floor. Like children again, the three Blue daughters. Charlotte was getting punished and the other two wanted to escape the line of fire but be close enough to get the scoop.

At thirty-two, Charlotte was living a child's life, sneaking around to find her way because her parents didn't trust her to make her own choices.

"To throw away a lucrative career for sex? For a tryst that won't go anywhere?" Tem said with a tsk of regret. "Amazingly foolish."

"There is no probationary term, is there? You want me off the staff now."

"I meant Nate Franco. The man who 'screwed up and

lost' you? Whittaker Doyle had practically groomed him to be his successor. Now he's gone. He quit."

Charlotte winced in surprise. A scuffle with Royce Davis and now this? What kind of game was Nate playing?

There was no time to even scratch the surface of his motives. The distaste in her parents' faces was a painful liberation. It was as if she'd been shoved into the sunshine after a lifetime of darkness. "You *are* bullies."

"Alessandro Franco—"

"I'm not talking about him," she interrupted Marshall. "I'm talking about me. The intimidation, the unfair way you handled the TreShawn Dibbs rumor, how you badger me into dates?" She sighed heavily. "Ma. Pop. I love and respect you both, but if some guy treated me the way you treat me, I would've dropped him by now."

Martha's gasp bubbled with laughter. "Sorry. Danni and I should leave."

"No, *I'm* leaving," Charlotte decided. "The villa. I'm moving out."

"Dramatics?" Tem said archly. "Do the adult thing—"

"I have been. You just don't approve of it. Fortunately, I do. I finally get that my own approval's all I need to be all right." Charlotte pointed to the glass panels. "I wanted to get on those sidelines more than I wanted my next meal. I have plans and proposals and hopes. But if caring about these players and being with a man who made me happier than I've been my entire adult life makes me an undesirable employee, then I'll take my talents elsewhere. Life will go on. It's kind of crazy that way."

Charlotte turned her back to the field and started for the door. "Whether I make it to your sidelines or not is up to you."

A decision came from the front office several days later. Charlotte had found a temporary place to crash on her best friend's couch and was devoting her every lunch break to house hunting in the city. She'd just returned to camp from a tour of a Fairway Pointe three-bedroom town house when her sister Danica entered the staff lounge.

With a single look, the woman cleared the room. Lockers slammed, papers were shuffled, footsteps pounded the floor as the other staff filed out of the lounge, leaving Charlotte alone with the woman who quite literally was holding Charlotte's fate in her hands.

Thankfully, Danica immediately gave her the sealed envelope and waited mutely as Charlotte tore it open and skimmed the official reprimand and what the punishment would be.

"Suspension." Charlotte looked to her sister.

"For the remainder of preseason. Effective end of day today." Danica gave her a considering look. "I'm going to ask you the tough questions, Charlotte. When did this… thing…with Nate Franco even start?"

"The night of the team party at the Bellagio. I met him at the Rio, didn't know who he was then."

"We were sorry to lose him. That kind of talent, those instincts don't come naturally to every trainer who makes it to the NFL."

"I don't like the idea that he quit so you and the owners would be forced to keep me on board."

"Good. Because the truth is, you would've been cut anyway, Charlotte, if the owners and I thought you weren't a valuable trainer. You deserve this shot. Kip and Whittaker tell me you have something that even Franco didn't have—fire. This is where you want to be, not where you think you want to be. There's a difference." Danica came over to stand beside her, nudging her gently with her elbow. "So, this thing with Nate. Was it just sex?"

Charlotte started to turn away, dodge the question that

would force her to confess aloud what she was trying so strongly to tamp down. Maybe if she ignored love, starved it, it would wither and she could shake off how much she missed Nate.

"Just say it," Danica urged, but her voice was soft with compassion.

"I love him. Crap, everything's so messed up."

"Not necessarily. The way I see it, you have until the season starts to get it together. I'll handle the media. You're going to come back to the Slayers ready to do what's best for this team. In the meantime, you'll do what's best for *you*."

When Danica left, Charlotte grabbed her cell phone. "Hi, roomie," she said when Joey answered. "A punishment's been handed down. I'm suspended for the rest of preseason."

"You're still gainfully employed," Joey reasoned. Then, "Let's celebrate. I know just the place."

After camp, Charlotte met her friend at UNLV's Bigelow Health Sciences Building and, crossing the parking lot to where Joey was carefully getting out of her car with her cane in tow, she said, "I thought you were kidding on the phone. Did you get us invited to a fraternity party?" A more serious thought occurred. "Are you about to bust a student?"

"No and no. We're sitting in on a lecture. See? Notebook, highlighters. And look—" she pointed at her hair gathered up with a pink scrunchie "—high ponytail. I'm all college-y. Don't leaving me hangin'."

Charlotte waited outside while Joey went into the building to confirm the location of the lecture she was bent on attending. Within ten minutes they were settling in the back row of a room with auditorium seating and a massive projection screen.

Students trooped in, chattering as they unzipped backpacks and powered down cell phones. Joey whispered, "I heard the guest lecturer is *muy caliente* and not such a bad guy."

A hot professor was something Charlotte's college experience lacked. When she told Joey so, her friend snorted. "Probably a good thing. I heard about your college shenanigans."

Charlotte muffled her giggle with a hand across her mouth. Then, when the class quieted and the lecturer took his place at the front of the room, she stopped laughing altogether.

Nate. She hardly heard his words as he dove into a lively presentation about forensic kinesiology. He spoke with a passion that gave her chills and with authority that captivated the class.

A sheet of notebook paper appeared in her periphery. Joey rolled a purple highlighter to her. Charlotte glanced at the all-caps note. *YOU'RE HOT FOR TEACHER.*

Charlotte's smile couldn't be stopped. She scribbled, *GUILTY.*

Joey scrawled something on the reverse side and slid the sheet over. *I WAS WRONG ABOUT HIM. I'M SORRY.*

When the students trickled out at the end of the lecture, Joey took her notebook and highlighter to the hallway and Charlotte moved quickly to the front of the room, where Nate was gathering his notes.

"Charlotte." He set down the pile of papers, crossed his arms, and she had to clear her throat to keep from sighing at how impressively his muscular form filled that textured striped shirt.

"Are you happy? Doing this, I mean?" she hastened to add, gesturing at their surroundings with the purple highlighter she'd forgotten to return to Joey. "Did you walk away from something you love just so I could keep my job?"

"You should be on that staff, Charlotte. But when I resigned, I walked *toward* something I love. I gave up doctoral study and teaching to be a part of my father's legacy. There's no legacy now. No reason to keep lying to myself and fighting for something I don't want."

"Teaching is what you want?"

"Yeah. But that's not all."

Tell me, Nate, and I'll know the truth.

Nate uncrossed his arms, raked a hand down from her shoulder to her fingertips, sending little shock waves through her. "I want you."

Charlotte swallowed. "Oh…okay, so…" Thinking fast, she grabbed the sheet of paper on the top of the pile and wiggled the highlighter. "Can I write on this?"

Puzzled, he gave a semblance of a nod.

"I'll call you on this date." As he frowned at what she jotted on the paper, she pressed, "Please. Want me enough to wait for me."

Charlotte hurried out of the room to where Joey waited near a cluttered bulletin board. "I have a date," she whispered as they started down the hall.

"Ooh! A new reason to celebrate. There's a drive-through cupcake joint downtown. We can rent a couple of *007* flicks, get a dozen cupcakes and be in sprinkle-and-frosting heaven by midnight."

"Or we can get the cupcakes and drop them off to Las Vegas's finest. I heard there's a *muy caliente* cop working the night shift."

Joey paused. "You're absolutely devious."

Grinning, Charlotte kept walking. "Thank you."

* * *

Charlotte had accepted her NFL penalty and the media backlash as fair, but now, as she sat on the edge of a stadium seat surrounded by excited football fans and the August-afternoon heat and watched the Slayers' kicker send the ball whizzing into the sky for a forty-eight-yard field goal—seven yards farther than his career record—she was itching to be free.

The official announced the kick as good as the stadium erupted in cheers, but with less than thirty game seconds left, the opposing team still dominated the scoreboard by a touchdown and the quarterback was taking a knee on the field, effectively running down the clock to secure a win.

The game clock rolled to 00:00 and Charlotte pumped her fist. Her suspension had just officially lifted.

She hurried to the sidelines to join the sea of players, staff and media personnel. "Congratulations on the field goal," she said, tapping TreShawn Dibbs on his shoulder, though she half expected him to ignore her.

TreShawn turned with a towel draped over his head, sized her up for a quick moment. "Thanks."

"I'll be going to Heaven and Hair for a trim soon. In case Georgiana or Boo asks if we're cool…?"

"We're cool, miss." And he gave her dap.

Anticipation built as Charlotte left the stadium. By the time she checked in at the Rio, got showered and dressed in the Cariocas Suite, she was heavy with eagerness. Confronting the mirror, she fussed with the ruffles on her plunging-neckline dress, applied lip gloss and, finally, picked up her cell phone.

"Charlotte." Nate's voice sizzled her nerve endings. "I said I'd call."

"I like how you say my name. I really like watching you say it."

Complete silence answered her. Then, "I can make that happen."

No going back now, Charlotte thought after she gave Nate her location, ended the call and set her phone to Do Not Disturb. No disruptions, no intrusions, no second-guessing. The last time she'd been in this suite, with Nate, life had interfered. She hadn't known him then, hadn't had an inkling of what they could mean to each other. She'd made the right decision to leave that night. But tonight... Tonight was theirs.

At the firm knock on the suite door, Charlotte turned away from the glimmering Las Vegas cityscape outside the windows. She silently congratulated herself for not swinging open the door and throwing herself at him. *Smooth, Charlotte, remember? Be smooth.*

Nate's gaze was a wave of heat that traveled from the softly curling dark hair hanging loose over her shoulder to the flirty ribbon straps of her high heels. "Damn."

Well, that could be interpreted a few different ways. "Uh...thanks?" she said, letting him into the suite. "Not too sure what you mean by that."

"I don't know what you mean by booking the Cariocas and inviting me here. We could hook up tonight, but where would that leave us tomorrow? Do you even forgive me for what happened with Bindi and that photo?"

Charlotte lifted the corner of her mouth in a smirk she knew was a one-two punch of smug and naughty. "Would I lure you to a hotel suite wearing no underwear whatsoever if I didn't forgive you?"

"Hell, yeah, you would. To punish me. To get me all hot for you, only to have you take off. You know that's torture, right?"

"Then you agree—we do have unfinished business." She walked backward and he matched her steps, maintaining the same close distance as they moved farther into the suite. She spun on her heel, indicating the mini basketball hoop that she'd hooked onto the master bedroom door. "We never did finish that B-ball game at camp."

Nate took a set of keys and his cell phone from his jeans pocket, dropped them onto the coffee table. One-handed, he grabbed the small-size basketball from the sofa and pointed it at the hoop. When he looked to her, his eyes were so dark, his stare so seeking. "How do you want to do this?"

She took the ball. "Hard. Fast."

"First to twenty-one?" He stripped off his checked overshirt to reveal the fitted gray tee beneath, and her body responded with something that felt a lot like hunger.

"Make it seven." Charlotte leaned to bounce the ball on the floor, her legs straight and the short dress inching up her thighs.

"Rules?" he asked, obviously admiring the shape of her butt.

"Full contact. Anything goes. But *do not* go easy on me."

"I won't if you won't."

Charlotte took the first shot, shoving hard against him in order to have an unobstructed drive to the hoop. But he recovered fast, snagged her around the waist, ruined her aim and caused the ball to strike the backboard. With a grunt she hit the wall of his body, and, using her position to his advantage, he gripped the nape of her neck and brought his hot mouth down on hers.

The kiss was fierce, almost violent. A promise and a plea. When he released her, she gasped to clear her head, then dove for the ball to secure the first point of the game.

He claimed the rebound and managed a bank shot even as she pushed up his shirt to drag her fingernails down his back. Determined, she grappled for the ball and sank a two-pointer.

In minutes the living area was hot, as heat rose up from their bodies to mingle in the humid air. Nate was a formidable opponent, but even in high heels with her hair in the way, Charlotte challenged him. With four points to his five, she bumped her body against his and yanked the ball free. Arms raised, she twirled away from him to shoot. But his arms circled her like steel bands, his hands closed possessively over her breasts and she whimpered with need as the ball escaped her grip.

Still, it dropped through the net, tying the game.

"Impressive," he acknowledged, swiping the rebound.

Charlotte was patient, letting him get all cocky as he showed off dribbling the mini basketball. At the precise moment that he moved in close for the next attempt, she dropped to her knees in front of him and within seconds had him going marble-hard in her hands.

"What are you doing?"

In response, Charlotte swept her tongue over her top lip. She was starving for him, for the future they could have together. "I'm waiting for you to score."

He let the ball fly. Another point for him.

Perspiration gleaming on her skin, she scrambled up for a desperate shot, only to miss. She rushed him, determined to block the shot that could give him victory. But, maybe in retaliation for her below-the-belt move, Nate used his body to hem her in with her back against the door, beneath the hoop.

Pressed against the door, Charlotte tangled her fingers in the net as she watched him lower before her. She shimmered in sweat, was beyond hot. Yet the feel of his lips, tongue and teeth on her flesh spiked her temperature.

Gripping the net with one hand and his head with the

other, Charlotte struggled to keep her eyes on Nate as her body weakened with spasms—one intense wave after another. "Wanting you—it's not enough. I tried to make it be enough. Loving you, being caught up in you, won't be easy, Nate."

"You don't want easy. You want hard. You want fast." Rising, he kissed up her sternum, nipping the swells of flesh exposed by the deep cut of her dress. "You want love, Charlotte. I love you."

That love was in the way he touched her, the way his gaze smoldered with it as he spoke her name.

Nate hauled her to him, then slammed the ball into the hoop with enough force to make the structure sing under the assault. Seven points.

Charlotte laughed, bowing up and wrapping him in an embrace with her arms, her legs…and her heart. "Game over."

* * * * *

In July, don't miss MIDNIGHT PLAY by Lisa Marie Perry. Book Two of THE BLUE DYNASTY features the passionate romance of Danica Blue and Dex Harper….

A sizzling new miniseries set in the wide-open spaces of Montana!

THE BROWARDS OF MONTANA
Passionate love in the West

JACQUELIN THOMAS	DARA GIRARD	HARMONY EVANS
Jacquelin Thomas	*Dara Girard*	*Harmony Evans*
Wrangling WES	**Engaging BROOKE**	**LOVING LANEY**

WRANGLING WES	ENGAGING BROOKE	LOVING LANEY
Available April 2014	*Available May 2014*	*Available June 2014*

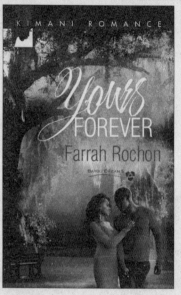